* * * *

OTHER BOOKS BY PAUL AUSTER

Poetry

Unearth
Wall Writing
Fragments from Cold
Facing the Music
Disappearances: Selected Poems 1970-1979

Novels

City of Glass
Ghosts
The Locked Room
In the Country of Last Things
Moon Palace
The Music of Chance
Leviathan
Mr. Vertigo

Non-fiction

White Spaces
The Invention of Solitude
The Art of Hunger
Why Write?
Hand to Mouth

Film

Smoke & Blue in the Face

Editor

The Random House Book
of Twentieth-Century French Poetry

TRANS LATIONS

PAUL AUSTER

MARSILIO PUBLISHERS: EW BOOKS
NEW YORK

English translations and Preface © 1997 Paul Auster

The Notebooks of Joseph Joubert © 1983 North Point Press
A Tomb for Anatole © 1983 North Point Press
On the High Wire © 1985 Random House
The Uninhabited © 1974 Living Hand

MARSILIO PUBLISHERS
853 Broadway
New York, NY 10003

ISBN 1-56886-033-1

Book and cover design by Drenttel Doyle Partners

Distributed in the U.S. by
Consortium Book Sales and Distribution
1045 Westgate Drive
Saint Paul, MN 55114

* * * *

ACKNOWLEDGEMENTS

Special thanks to André du Bouchet and Philippe Petit for their comments on the translations; to Claude Royet-Journoud, Mary Ann Caws, Jonathan Galassi, Eliot Weinberger, and Jack Shoemaker for help and encouragement along the way; and a large debt of gratitude to Chris Tysh for changes and improvements in the Mallarmé translation. *A Tomb for Anatole* has been substantially revised for this edition.

P. A.

CONTENTS

TRANS
LATIONS

* * * *

INTRODUCTION

This book is a quadruple reprint, a simultaneous resurrection of four works I have admired and cared about for more than half my life. Each one represents a passionate discovery for me, and each translation was a labor of love, an attempt to share my enthusiasm for these writings with the world at large. In their first incarnations, they all existed as separate books, but those editions are now out of print. Three of the original prefaces resurfaced in a collection of essays I published several years ago,* but the translations themselves have been unavailable for more than a decade. To see them born again makes me feel like a proud father.

It is an odd assortment, I suppose. Written variously in the eighteenth, nineteenth, and twentieth centuries, the books themselves will strike many people as odd as well. Two of them consist of nothing more than notes and were published posthumously. In some sense, they are not really books at all. Another one of the writers is not, strictly speaking, a writer, and yet his book is

*The Art of Hunger (Sun & Moon Press, 1992; Penguin Books, 1993).

probably the most literary of the four. Joseph Joubert and Stéphane Mallarmé are long dead; André du Bouchet and Philippe Petit are very much alive. Two are poets; one is a writer who never produced a book; the last is a performer. For all their many differences, however, I believe it makes sense to publish these books together—and not just because they were all translated by the same person.

Joseph Joubert (1754-1824) spent his entire adult life recording his thoughts and ideas in notebooks. At first, he looked upon these jottings as a way to prepare himself for a larger, more systematic work, a great book of philosophy that he dreamed he had it in him to write. As the years passed, however, and the great project continued to elude him, he slowly came to realize that the notebooks were an end in themselves. By 1804, he was able to admit that "These thoughts form not only the foundation of my work, but of my life." It wasn't until 1838 that excerpts from the notebooks were first published (in an edition prepared by Chateaubriand, Joubert's close friend). Another one hundred years went by before the complete notebooks were issued in a two-volume set, scrupulously edited by Andre Beaunier. It was this 1938 edition that I used in making my selections.

Except for his correspondence, the nine hundred tightly-printed pages of *Les Carnets* represent Joubert's entire output as a writer. They reveal a man of the utmost discretion and honesty, a thinker of such plain-spoken brilliance that one winds up embracing him as a friend. Joubert was not a writer of maxims in the traditional French manner. Everything is mixed together in the notebooks, and reflections on writing, literature, and philosophy are scattered among observations about the weather, the landscape, family, society, and politics. The humdrum and the sublime co-exist. Entries of unforgettable psychological insight ("Those who never back down love themselves more than they love the truth") alternate with brief, chilling comments on the revolutionary turmoil around him ("Stacking the dead on top of each other"), which in turn are punctuated by sudden outbursts of levity ("They say that souls have no sex; of course they do"). The more you read Joubert, the more you trust him, and however remote his era might feel to us now, his voice has a distinctly modern sound to it. No one paid any attention to Joubert during his lifetime, but he still speaks to us, while most of his contemporaries do not.

When my translation was first published in 1983, this fact was brought home to me in a rather extraordinary way. I gave a copy of the book to one of my friends. This friend had a friend who had recently landed in Bellevue after suffering a nervous breakdown. When he went to visit him in the hospital, he left behind his copy of Joubert — on loan. Two or three weeks later, when my friend's friend was finally released, he called my friend to apologize for not returning the book. After he had read it, he said, he had given it to another patient. That patient had passed it on to yet another patient, and little by little Joubert made his way around the ward. Interest in the book became so keen that groups of patients would get together in the day room and read passages out loud to one another. When my friend's friend asked for the book back, he was told that it no longer belonged to him. "It's our book," one of the patients said. "We need it." As far as I am concerned, this is the most eloquent literary criticism I have ever heard, proof that the right book in the right place is medicine for the human soul. As Joubert himself put it in an entry from 1801: "A thought is a thing as real as a cannon ball."

Both Georges Poulet and Maurice Blanchot, two of France's leading critics, have suggested that Joubert's writings anticipate
Mallarmé's poetic enterprise half a century later. In his essay, *Joubert
and Space*, Blanchot goes so far as to draw explicit parallels between the two men and notes the feeling shared by both Joubert
and Mallarmé, "that literature and poetry are the locus of a secret
that should perhaps be put before everything else, even the glory of
making books."

Mallarmé (1842-1898) requires no introduction, but because
of the difficulties of translating his work into English, he is generally
regarded as a distant, even glacial figure, an almost disembodied
presence dwelling among the ethers of Mount Parnassus, a man so
dedicated to the pursuit of his art that he is all but unknowable as
a man. When I stumbled across *Pour un tombeau d'Anatole* in
1971, this view of Mallarmé was suddenly overturned for me. From
that moment on, I have seen him in an utterly different light.

The book is a compilation of notes and fragments written by
the poet in 1879, immediately before and after the death of his
eight-year-old son, Anatole. Clearly, Mallarmé had a project in
mind—a tomb of words, a literary monument that would wrest
some meaning from the death of the beloved boy. He never got
very far with it. He scribbled down his thoughts on little scraps of
paper and put them in a box. They remained unknown to the world
until 1961, when critic and scholar Jean-Pierre Richard deciphered,
edited, and published them in an elaborately annotated book. Not
only do the fragments show us an entirely different Mallarmé from
the Mallarmé of legend—a grieving, devastated father, a man racked
with torment and sorrow—but studded in the notes themselves are

moments of unsurpassed beauty and intimacy, an altogther new poetic language. The elaborate, highly constructed syntax of Mallarmé's poems gives way to a chopped-up, telegraphic style—a grammar of sobs, impulses, and darting images. It would be an exaggeration to call them poems, perhaps, but reading these cryptic utterances today, at the end of the twentieth century, they seem closer to what we consider to be poetry than they did at the time they were written. However you want to define them, these fragments offer a startling glimpse of a great poet's mind at work. They are also among the most heartbreaking pages I have ever read.

André du Bouchet (born in 1924) is widely regarded as one of the most radical and innovative French poets of the post-War generation. I discovered his work as a student in the sixties, and the translations in *The Uninhabited* are among the first I ever did. At the time they were finished (1971), they could be legitimately described as the "selected poems of. . .", but that is no longer the case. There were just two du Bouchet collections back then (*Dans La Chaleur Vacante*, 1961, and *OU LE SOLEIL*, 1968), but he has since gone on to publish numerous other books, which means that my efforts should now be read as no more than a small sampling of his early work. What impressed me about that work when I was twenty, and what still impresses me about it now, is the absolute singularity of du Bouchet's universe. His poems sound like no one else's poems. In the context of the French poetic tradition—with its tendency toward rhetorical excess and abstraction—they qualify as acts of sabotage. The bombast has been deflated, the lofty tropes have been sent crashing to the ground, and it is as if we were starting all over again, as if the whole idea of poetry had to be reinvented from the bottom up. Sparse and elegant, devoid of metaphor, du Bouchet's poems are situated in a landscape of elemental simplicity, and they speak in the rhythms of the body, the cadences of the human breath. It would be hard to find an equivalent approach to writing among contemporary American poets, but if one thinks of Robert Creeley, say, or George Oppen, or perhaps even Larry Eigner, one would begin to have some sense of the nature of du Bouchet's project. Another way to think about it would be to consider the sculptures of Alberto Giacometti. Du Bouchet and Giacometti were close friends, and in addition to his work as a poet and translator (of Shakespeare, Hölderlin, Joyce, among others), du Bouchet has written extensively about Giacometti's art. There is an undeniable kinship between them. The "I" in du Bouchet's poems bears a close resemblance to one of Giacometti's walking men—those lean, stripped-down figures striding forward through space—always on the brink of taking the next step, of drawing the next breath. A similar drama plays itself out in these poems. There is no story told in them, no point to be proved, no moral lesson to be learned. What they recount is the adventure of a man standing alone in his own skin, the experience of being alive.

Philippe Petit (born in 1949) was twenty-three years old when he wrote *On the High Wire*. That is an early age for any writer to finish his first book, but when one stops and considers who the writer is—and why he wrote the book in the first place—the achievement becomes even more impressive. Philippe Petit is the most celebrated high-wire walker in the world. He has been performing feats of aerial magic for more than twenty-five years now, and to find a figure of comparable importance in the annals of that dangerous art, one would have to go all the way back to Blondin in the nineteenth century.

In America, Petit is best remembered as the man who walked between the towers of the World Trade Center in 1974, dancing on his wire for more than an hour as crowds of astonished New Yorkers gathered below. He was arrested for that illegal performance, as he was in 1971 for walking between the towers of Notre Dame Cathedral in Paris and in 1973 for causing similar mayhem in Sidney, Australia. Since those early days of his career, he has largely worked with the sanction of the authorities, putting on spectacles in such far-flung cities as Jerusalem, Tokyo, and Vienna. In 1989, as part of the French Bicentennial festivities in Paris, he dazzled a crowd of several hundred thousand people by walking on an inclined cable between the Palais de Chaillot and the second story of the Eiffel Tower. Even now, he is plotting future performances, preparing himself for even greater challenges. Among them: a high-wire opera above the Little Colorado River in the Grand Canyon (1800 feet off the ground) and a mile-long walk over Niagara Falls.

Given the scope of these accomplishments, it is almost unthinkable that Philippe Petit should also be a writer. As far as I know, there are no precedents for a book like *On the High Wire*. It is rare enough for a performer of Petit's caliber to have such a conscious grasp of the thing he does, but to be able to articulate his thoughts in such lucid well-turned prose, to have penetrated the spiritual implications of his art with such refinement is surely unheard of. *On the High Wire* is not an autobiography, a "how-to-book," or an account of show business adventures. It is the work of a young philosopher-poet trying to delineate the map of his inner world. It is by turns arrogant and humble, idealistic and practical, and everywhere informed by a fierce, burning intelligence. High-wire walking would seem to be an essentially physical skill, a matter of learning how to control the body under perilous circumstances. Philippe

Petit teaches us that it is also a question of mind, of gaining mastery over one's soul.

It is not difficult for me to remember what attracted me to these four books when I first read them. Not only was each one different from every other book I had read, but the newness in them felt necessary to me, a product of earnest struggle in the trenches of life and not just some desire to make "literature." Each one of these writers speaks in his own way, but there are resonances among them, shared qualities that allow them to stand comfortably together in a single book: rigor of thought, intensity of purpose, courage. Their sensibilities complement one another, and in a surprising number of instances, their ideas intersect. The links between Joubert and Mallarmé have already been noted, but similar connections could also be made between Mallarmé and du Bouchet. Comb through Joubert's notebooks, and you will find an entry from 1798 that could easily serve as an epigraph for Philippe Petit's treatise on high-wire walking, written in 1972: "Man feels that his happiness is in the air." Air is a preoccupation for all of these writers, a theme that runs through their work with remarkable consistency. Air as breath, air as space, air as light—which makes the world visible. It is the primordial element, the source.

Before I settled on the title *Translations*, I thought of calling this book *Skywriting*. When all is said and done, it would have made just as much sense.

P.A.
March 1996

* * * *

Joseph Joubert

Notebooks: A Selection

* * * *

[1783]

The only way to have friends is to throw everything out the window, to keep your door unlocked, and never to know where you will be sleeping at night.

You will tell me there are few people mad enough to act like this. Well then, they shouldn't complain about not having any friends. They don't want any.

Do you want to know how thought functions, to know its effects? Read the poets. Do you want to know about morality, about politics? Read the poets. What pleases you in them, deepen: it is the truth.

In order to write perfectly, one must write and think in the same way a perfect man would write and think at the moment when all the faculties of his being were in perfect harmony. This situation would be possible in some state of soul in which all the passions were developed in all their force and to their full extent and combined in perfect equilibrium.

It is up to poets to form languages and up to philosophers to reform them. How many words are wrong! And if the accumulation of discoveries each generation must pass on to the next were as vast as it could be, every language would undergo a revolution every hundred years.

In France we seem to like the arts more to judge them than to enjoy them.

I am trying to figure out what place women should occupy in the republic. We have made a sort of property out of them. Is this dominion just? I remind myself of the principle I established earlier: "whenever an institution destroys a single right of a single person, this institution is bad."

Men are children. They must be pardoned for everything, except malice.

During the rain there is a certain darkness that stretches out all objects. Beyond that, its effect on our body forces us to withdraw into ourselves, and this inwardness makes our soul infinitely more sensitive. The very noise rain produces, which the Latins called *densissimus imber*, continuously occupies the ear, awakes attentiveness and keeps us on the alert. The brownish hue the moisture gives to the walls, the trees, the rocks, adds to the impression these objects make. And the solitude and silence it spreads out around the traveler, by forcing animals and men to be quiet and to seek shelter, makes these impressions more distinct. Enveloped in his coat, his head covered, and moving along deserted paths, the traveler is struck by everything, and everything is enlarged before his imagination or his eyes. The streams are swollen, the grass is thicker, the stones are more sharply defined; the sky is closer to the earth, and all objects, closed up in this narrowed horizon, occupy a greater space and importance.

What makes the waters consoling is their movement and their limpidity. . . .

When a nation gives birth to an individual capable of producing a great thought, another is born who is capable of understanding and admiring it.

If I die and leave several scattered thoughts on important things, I beg in the name of humanity that those who see what has been left suppress nothing that seems at odds with accepted ideas. During my life I loved only the truth. I feel I have seen it in many great things. Perhaps one of these [words?] that I have dashed off in haste . . .

[1784]

If the earth must perish, then astronomy is our only consolation.

[1785]

I imitate the dove, and often I throw a blade of grass to the drowning ant.

[1786]

O my friends! I have drunk love . . .

Nota. Socrates had observed (*sic*) that to taste wines properly we must sip them while drinking. A lesson of pleasure and temperance! . . .

If curiosity had not made us examine the nature of plants, how they take root, how they grow, how they die, how they reproduce . . . we would enjoy their fruits no more fully than animals do, and perhaps with even less pleasure. . . .

If there is one sad thing in the world, it is the poplar on the mountains. . . .

Every sound in music must have an echo; every figure must have a sky in painting; and we who sing with thoughts and paint with words, every sentence and each word in our writings must also have its horizon and its echo.

Thought forms in the soul in the same way clouds form in the air.

[1787]

A work of genius, whether poetic or didactic, is too long if it cannot be read in one day.

Apparent extension of the fields on Sunday. Born of two causes:

absence of sounds and absence of visible objects.

Noise that comes from a single place makes the places around it seem deserted. When it comes from several, it makes even the intervals seem populated.

It is to the mind, to the soul even more than to the eye, that the countryside seems extended, immense, uninhabited.

The silence of the fields. How everything hushes imperceptibly with the fall of night. How everything seems to be gathered up: men and animals, by the work of unanimous silence; plants and all things that move, for the wind falls when evening comes near, and the air holds only a single, frail breath. It is from this immobility of all things, and because the remaining light is reflected more during these tranquil hours by the earth and its rocks than by the trees and plants, that the hills and fields seem to lift up the earth and to stand in wonder.

Sad harvests . . .

The essential thing is not that there be many truths in a work, but that no truth be abused.

[1789]

——There is no more white paper on the earth and the source of ink has dried up.—Give my pen an iron point, a diamond point, give me leaves of copper; I will engrave on them. . . .—

It is not facts, but rumors that cause emotions among the people. What is believed creates everything.

Extension is the body of God, as Newton would readily say.

Mixture of dry and wet. Water swells before boiling.

[1790]

The ears and eyes are the doors and windows of the soul.

. . . And travel through open spaces where one sees nothing but light . . . *Like Plato.*

. . . They are born old . . .

[1791]

Inundation. The Seine wanted to see the Bastille destroyed. It invoked the waters of heaven, and the waters of heaven carried it to the foot of the walls, where those famous towers once reigned, and which the inhabitants of Paris leveled to the ground three times three months and nine days ago.

Are you listening to the ones who keep quiet?

A winter without cold and without fire.

Always to link unknown things to known things.

The republic is the only cure for the ills of the monarchy, and the monarchy is the only cure for the ills of the republic.

. . . where the accusers are almost always the guilty ones.

The reading of Plato is like mountain air. It does not nourish, but it sharpens our faculties and gives us a taste for fine food.

Through memory we travel against time, through forgetfulness we follow its course.

In these times of trouble, one commits and suffers great evil.

Everything that has wings is beyond the reach of the laws.

——*Nota.* We must do as much to read an abbreviation as to read a word written in its entirety. This is because it is the mind that reads and not simply the eyes.

We are in the world as words are in a book. Each generation is like a line, a phrase.

Writing is closer to thinking than to speaking.

The cock sings the hours. It has sung midnight.

[1793]

Wisdom is the strength of the weak.

His ink has the colors of the rainbow.

Let heaven forgive the wicked, after they have been punished.

In order to live, we need little life. In order to love, we need much.

It is necessary that something be sacred.

The good is worth more than the best.

What makes civil wars more murderous than other wars is that we can more easily accept having a stranger for an enemy than a neighbor; we do not want to keep the possibility of vengeance so near.

A sluggish river that carries nothing.

Imitate time. It destroys slowly. It eats away, it uses up, it uproots, it detaches and does not rip apart.

In their words one hears the tinkling of their brains.

We need a ladder to the mind. A ladder and rungs.

[1794]

Here is the desert. In this silence everything speaks to me: and in your noise everything falls silent.

Freedom. That is to say, independence of one's body.

The number of books is infinite.

* * *My son was born during the night of the 8th and 9th, at two and a quarter hours past midnight.

That he one day remember the pains of his mother!

* * *we gave the child his names. It was the wise woman who named him, beside the fire, at three o'clock in the afternoon.

He is named *Victor Joseph*, after his mother and myself.

That same day I heard the nightingale.

I thought of my own happiness, of the mother's calm and peace in body and soul, of the fine and decent shape of the child, which is an inestimable good. Though born of a weak mother he is quite strong. His constitution is healthy. He came into this world at Lacédémone. The child and mother are doing well. After so many fears concerning them both, such happily demented fears, I told myself *rejoice*.

I stayed at home and walked in the little garden to be alone in my joy.

Labor was never happier, nursing never less difficult.

The child does not seem wicked.

* * *The gray bird
in the Chaumont woods.

The mother got out of bed. Her thinness is considerable. The child nursed the whole time she was carrying him.

Today he opened his eyes more often and longer than usual. He even seemed to want to smile when his aunt tickled him.

Of the last word.—The last word must be the last. It is like a last hand that puts the last nuance on a color, nothing can be added to it.

Nuance on nuance—in this way color is formed.

Transparency on transparency.

Big words. Claim too much attention.

Eye—is the sun of the face.

The sieve of forgetfulness. Or the riddle of forgetfulness.

Or: Memory and forgetfulness are the mother and father of the muses. True knowledge is composed of these two things. Or: it holds a riddle in its hand. This riddle is called forgetfulness.

The soul paints itself in our machines.

Tragedy and marionettes. The strings. Undoing the strings. The ropes.

All truths are double or doubled, or they all have a front and a back.

Soul.—It is a lit vapor that burns without consuming itself. Our body is its lantern. Etc. The flame of this vapor is not only light but feeling. Etc.

I have little sap. Etc.

They cannot accustom themselves to lacking nothing.

Prescience. Is it possible?

[1795]

Children must have stories.
    Children: who cannot speak. In talking to them, we soften our voice. We lower its volume, its range, etc.

The sun is clipped. Fogs.
Nota. Hair, like rays.
Fogs that dust the trees.

Roundness. This shape guarantees matter a long life. Time does not know where to take hold of it.

These *coups d'état* are necessary, you tell me. I answer you, what is sinister and criminal is never necessary at any time.

One writes with a pen, the other writes with a brush.

Children always want to look behind mirrors.

Imitate the spinner. Imitate the ant. One gathers during the summer what is necessary in winter, and the other prepares in winter what is necessary in summer.

Nimbleness. Agility of mind. These works are no more than perilous leaps into space.

Dreams. Their lantern is magical.

Love and fear. Everything the father of a family says must inspire one or the other.

Light. It is a fire that does not burn.

A tact placed before us and outside us.—An inner tact.

[1796]

The ancients knew about anatomy only through war. It was on the battlefields that they learned all they knew about it.

The splendor of fire. The word *clangor* for sound answers that of *splendor* for light.

In these times when minds are not calm.

Twenty-five-thousand-four-hundred-sixty-nine laws! . . .

The beauties of transition and those of isolation.

Passions come like a smallpox and disfigure this original beauty.

The people. They know how to know, but not how to choose.

He must confess his darknesses.

I will build a temple for the worship of dreams.

Give me a morality that equally suits the healthy and the sick, men and women, children, adults, and old people.

Everything that cannot grow diminishes, even the qualities that are passed on. Is this true?

An age in which we have children who can scarcely remember having seen their fathers.

The first part and last part of human life are what is best about it, or at least what is most respectable. The one is the age of innocence, the other is the age of reason. You must write for these two ages and banish from your mind and your books that which does not suit one or the other.

I love to see two truths at the same time. Every good comparison gives the mind this advantage.

. . . His necessity invincibly proves his existence.

Illusion is in sensations. Error is in judgments. We can know truth and at the same time take pleasure in illusion.

One loves to say what he knows, and the other to say what he thinks.

Pleasures are always children, pains always have wrinkles.

The imagination is the eye of the soul.

There are truths that cannot be apprehended in conversation.

Forbidden to speak of God . . .

What comes through war is given back through war. All spoils will be retaken, all plunder will be dispersed. All victors will be defeated and every city filled with prey will be sacked in its turn.

With the telescope, with the microscope, we have seen a great number of phenomena; and that is all.

Plato. He is an author whose ideas cannot be understood until they have become our own.

Take us back to the time when wine was invented. . . .

The penchant for destruction is one of the ways used for conserving the world.

Divorce. Its existence and use should be determined only by the interests of the children.

We must give reasons to people that are not only good for us but good for them as well.

The hordes of words that fill our books proclaim our ignorance, reveal the obscurities that flood our knowledge. If we were perfectly enlightened, our moral books would contain only maxims and our books on physics and spirituality would contain only axioms and facts. Everything else is clutter and shows no more than our gropings, our efforts, and our difficulties.

Deism. The human species cannot accommodate itself to it. This doctrine relates to our strengths but not to our weaknesses.

Illusion is an integral part of reality. It is an essential presence, in the same way an effect is essential to a cause. (Integral part, which means a part without which a thing does not have the whole integrity of its constitution or application, etc.)

Fathers love their children because they are theirs. The more a child becomes the property of his father through the law, the more he will be loved. For the happiness of the children themselves paternal authority must be given great scope and weight.

Nevertheless, a child should not be his father's thing, as Diderot understood it, but he should be his person, in brief, he should belong to him to the extent that one human being can belong to another.

Models.—There are no more models.

When a thought gives birth to obscurity, it must be rejected, renounced, abandoned.

God is the place where I do not remember the rest.

[1797]

In order to be known, he would have to make us immortal and give us another life.

There is a class of society in which pious children do not know their parents are mortal. They have never dared to think about it.

We cannot imagine the *all* as having form, for every form is but the visible and palpable difference of the object that is clothed by it.

To compensate absence with memory.

A flower that cannot bloom, a bud that cannot open.

To seek wisdom rather than truth. It is more within our grasp.

Chance is a role that providence has reserved for itself in the affairs of the world, a role through which it could make certain that men would feel they have no influence.

Anger makes us adroit.

Democracy and slavery inseparable. Why.
    Democracy as it existed among the ancients was no more than government by a number of men large enough to be called the people. But this designation is false. The true people, in such a state, the greatest number, the majority belong to the class of slaves, and slavery inevitably develops in a country governed in this way, because it is impossible that those who spend their time making laws can make shoes and clothes, plant crops, work fields, etc.

The mind can only create errors. Truths are not created, they exist; one can only see them, disentangle them, discover them, and expose them.

Lovers. Whoever does not have their weaknesses cannot have their strengths.

Clarity of mind is not given in all centuries.

We do not write our books in advance, we do them as we write them. What is best about our works is hidden by scaffoldings: our texts are filled with what must be kept and what must be left behind.

They do not know how to apply names to things.

Forgetfulness of all earthly things, desire for heavenly things, immunity from all intensity and all disquiet, from all cares and all worries, from all trouble and all effort, the plenitude of life without agitation. The delights of feeling without the work of thought. The ravishments of ecstasy without medication. In a word, the happiness of pure spirituality in the heart of the world and amidst the tumult of the senses. It is no more than the gladness of an hour, a minute, an instant. But this instant, this minute of piety spreads its sweetness over our months and our years.

Yes, the soul must breathe. This wave is its air, its space. Within it, it can move at will. A single bit (*haustus*) of this element is enough to refresh, it contains the principle of its well-being— which is the effect of its moderations.

In metaphysics, the art of writing consists of making sensible and palpable what is abstract. To make abstract what is palpable is its vice and fault. It is the fault of those we have so mistakenly called metaphysicians in this century.

We have the memory of individuals, but we do not have the idea. We have the idea of qualities and cannot have a memory of them. Memory is the representation of fixed and determined figures. The idea cannot. . .

What our eyes see, our imagination can no longer see. The same things cannot be the object of both kinds of seeing.

For our entire lives we are for moral things what children are for physical things, wanting to join enormously disproportionate things to each other, to adjust big clothes to little bodies and long shoes to little feet.

A sensibility that overflows; that is to say, it spreads beyond its canal and is not held back by the dikes of reason. It floods all objects and fills the head as well as the heart.

Perfection is composed of minute things. It is ridiculous to put them aside and not to use them.

The exclusive study of natural history bends us constantly toward the earth. The mind no longer lifts its eyes.

The imagination has made more discoveries than the eye.

Psalms. Read them with the intention of praying and you will find them beautiful. Eh! Doesn't every reading demand a readiness of mind that is special and appropriate to it?

Life is born in the same way as fire, from friction. Moisture and fire are not incompatible.
    Life spreads into all places. All space is filled with it. Like fire, it is kindled, it flares, and is fixed by being joined to the individual, like fire when it consumes a candle.

Why do I get so tired when I speak? Because, when I speak, a part of my strength is exerting itself while the other part is inactive; the part that is acting alone supports the difficulty and the weight of the action and is soon overwhelmed. This unequal distribution of forces in me leads to an unequal distribution of activity in all my parts. Therefore: total fatigue when the strong part is fatigued, because then the weakness is everywhere.

When men are imbeciles, the one who is mad dominates the others.

The tomb swallows us, but it does not digest us. We are consumed but not destroyed.

God made life to be lived (the world to be inhabited) and not to be known.

The thoughts about which we can say: "There is rest in this thought." This image is encouraging.

This world seems to me a whirlwind inhabited by a people whose head keeps turning and turning.

The dying inherit the dead.

Imprisoned in our body . . . and our soul has its windows.

Don't cut what you can untie.

Sacred language. It should be hieroglyphical. All words should seem hollowed out or in relief, chiseled or sculpted. Black and white, emptiness and fullness are suitable to it. Everything must be juxtaposed and united, but separated by intervals.

The intellectual world is always the same. It is just as easy to know it today as it was in the beginning, and it was just as hidden in the beginning as it is today.

To create the world, a speck of matter was enough, for every-thing we see, this mass that frightens us, is no more than a speck that eternity has set in motion. Through its malleability, through the hollows it closes up and the art of the worker who did the work, this speck offers a kind of immensity in the embellishments that emerge from it. A speck of gold will explain us, etc.

Everything seems full to us; everything is empty, or, to be more exact, everything is hollow.—Everything is hollow; and the elements themselves are hollow. God alone is full.
　　—Penetrable bodies are more hollow than the others.

　　　　　　　　　　　　　　　(

"Yes, please cut up the pieces for me," he said, "but don't chew them."

It is a drop of breathed water, a speck of flattened metal.

Thought is not a greater marvel than thinking. Nor, perhaps, does it demand an immateriality that is any purer. Both operate through representations made by the inner mirrors that our inner sight is constantly looking into.

Do not say the word that completes the symmetry of your sentence and rounds it off when the reader will inevitably think of it and say it to himself after having read the words that precede it.

Intimate interior evidence. Clarity without any flash. Built by the ease of belief. The *invidence*, if such a word can be used.

Our arms are canes of flesh with which the soul reaches and touches.

In a grain of sand there is fire, water, air, and dust.

The air itself is only the body of another, far more subtle air.
    To change my diamonds into pearls . . .

The weakness of the dying slanders life.

Do not:—Define what is known: gossip. Obscure what is clear: scribbling. Question what exists: bad faith, ignorance. Make

abstract what is palpable: charlatanism. Present difficulties that
are not there or are only apparent: deceit.

Tell me what is happening on earth.

All these philosophers are no more than surgeons.

Resignation is a hundred times easier than courage, for it has a
motive outside of us and courage does not. If both diminish evils,
let us use the one that diminishes it the most. (Outside us, that is
to say beyond our will.)

Remember to let your ink grow ripe.

The shifting path of the waters . . .
A river of air and light . . .
Folds of clarity . . .

Sexes. One has the look of a wound, the other of
something skinned.

Matter is a part of itself that is beyond itself.

Where do thoughts go? Into the memory of God.

Beautiful enclosures please us because they clearly print in us the idea of a portion of space; just as a beautiful harmony makes us feel spontaneously and unconsciously the movement and repose that are the elements of time.

God's light goes to the stars and from the stars to us.

Delicate minds are all sublimely born minds that have not been able to take flight, because of weak organs, or erratic health, or because lazy habits have held them back.

The world was populated by artists who limited themselves to painting society as they found it and let everything stay as it was, whether beautiful or flawed. They are followed by true masons who want to rebuild it.

The staircase that leads us to God. What does it matter if it is make-believe, if we really climb it? What difference does it make who builds it, or if it is made of marble or wood, of brick, stone, or mud? The essential thing is that it be solid and that in climbing it we feel the peace that is inaccessible to those who do not climb it.

Around every flame there must be a void, so there can be light. Without space, no light.

[1798]

What is a diamond, if not a bit of gleaming mud?

One can be stingy with words, but not stingy with syllables.

Nothing is perfect on this earth. Even piety is imperfect. Even the piety of saints.

Images have had a great influence on realities.

The sign then makes us forget the thing signified.

What good is modesty?—It makes us seem more beautiful when we are beautiful, and less ugly when we are ugly.

Beauties that leave nothing to the imagination.

To hide our eyes to make others believe we are hiding tears.

The truth. They make it consist of nothing they cannot prove. The greatest happiness they find in it is being able to put forward incontestable assertions. This is what they like, and they consider it a sign of prestige, a prerogative, a power, a dignity, etc., a liberation from error.

Illusion. God created it and placed it between the seeds, the fruits, flesh, and the palace of the mouth, and from this tastes were born; between the flowers and their smells, and from this perfumes were born; between hearing and sounds, and from this was born harmony, melody, etc., between the eyes and objects, and from this were born colors, perspective, beauty.

It is a small bit of nature that amuses itself by giving us pleasure through evaporation.

It is different from error. If I see colors without seeing any object, as in the air for example, I am in error. In the opposite case, I am under an illusion and still within the truth.

All illusion is produced by some emanation and is the effect of a cloud, a vapor, the intervention of a fluid. If the organ is tainted, if the object is improperly disposed or altered in its constituent parts, there is no illusion. One of the two parts is then lacking to set the process in motion, and the play of illusion can no longer work.

Illusions. They can thus be produced only by these effluvia, these invisible outflows, these subtle emanations that maintain the perpetual currents between these different beings. They cannot therefore give and receive agreeable sensations if they do not somewhere produce some loss of substance. Thus, to the condition of change and decline is attached the good of inspiring and feeling pleasure.

The breath of God. God created everything with his breath.

Nothing in the moral world is lost, just as nothing in the material world is annihilated. All our feelings and thoughts on this earth are only the beginnings of feelings and thoughts that will be completed elsewhere.

The only good in man is his young feelings and his old thoughts.

Stars more beautiful to the eye than to the telescope that robs them of their illusions.

Music, perspective, architecture, etc. Embroider time, embroider space.

To draw up in advance an exact and detailed plan is to deprive our mind of the pleasures of the encounter and the novelty that comes from executing the work. It is to make the execution insipid for us and consequently impossible in works that depend on enthusiasm and imagination. Such a plan is itself a half-work. It must be left imperfect if we want to please ourselves. We must say it cannot be finished. In fact it must not be, for a very good reason: it is impossible. We can, however, draw up such plans for works whose execution and accomplishment are a mechanical thing, a thing that depends above all on the hand. This is suitable and even very useful for painters, for sculptors. Their senses, with each stroke of the brush or chisel, will find this novelty that did not exist for their minds. Forms and colors, which the imagination cannot represent to us as perfectly as the eye can, will offer the artist a horde of these encounters which are indispensable to giving genius pleasure in work. But the orator, the poet, and the philosopher will not find the same encouragement in writing down what they have already thought. Everything is one for them. Because the words they use have beauty only for the mind and, having been spoken in their head in the same way they are written on the page, the mind no longer has anything to discover in what it wants to say. A plan however is necessary, but a plan that is vague, that has not been pinned down. We must above all have a notion of the beginning, the end, and the middle of our work. That is to say, we must choose its pitch and range, its pauses, and its objectives. The first word must give the color, the beginning determines the tone; the middle rules the measure, the time, the space, the proportions.

. . . This spark that unexpectedly fell on my childhood and burned my entire youth.

In the same way that man was made in the image of God, the earth was made in the image of heaven.

. . . Pleasure of being seen from afar.

A century in which the body has become subtle, in which the mind has become coarse.

One fills himself only with juices, warm waters, vapors, lightnesses. The other concerns himself only with matter, animals, minerals, configurations, and weights. Bodies that receive an over-subtle nourishment and minds concerned only with objects that are too real and too hard, are equally depraved.

They have an earthly mind with airy bodies.

To live without sky. . .

To reason, to argue. It is to walk with crutches in search of the truth. We come to it with a leap. We must use reasoning to make sure we have reached the end and that we have covered the whole path. Likewise in the stadium, the runner touches the stone with his hands and steps back to see the barrier in front of the goal.

These false rules only serve to persuade those who observe them that they have attained what they cannot attain.

We have led our minds astray. . . .

Among the three extensions, we must include time, space, and silence. Space is in time, silence is in space.

To be in one's place, to be at one's post, to be part of the order, to be content. Not to murmur of suffering, to be incapable of being unhappy.

Too much talk (they say). *Nota bene*: too much writing.

It is impossible to love the same person twice.

That peace is the object of morality and politics. Peace with one-self, peace between citizens, peace between the city and strangers.

This life: the cradle of our existence.—What do they matter then—sickness, time, old age, death—which are merely the various degrees of a metamorphosis that perhaps only begins here on earth. Alas! these clarities escape us! and this is one of the insurmountable fatalities of our present lot. I would like to be able to remember, however, in that far-distant future, all the fugitive moments of my present life which by then will have been in the eternal past for such a long time. The ones who will be happiest are those who will not have a single moment from their lives that cannot be represented distinctly and with pleasure in memory.—There as here our memories (which will be sharp) will make up the better part of what is good and bad in us. This very moment that I am speaking to you, this moment in which I am saying this, will be repeated forever. Man lets time get lost, but there are no lost moments.

The cry of the chimney sweep; the song of the cricket.

Strength without repose (in Lavater).—Forces always at work, an activity without rest, movement without intervals, agitation without calm, passions without melancholy, pleasures without tranquility. It is to live without ever sitting down, to grow old standing up, to banish slumber from life and to die without ever having slept.

To think what we do not feel is to lie to ourselves, in the same way that we lie to others when we say what we do not think. Everything we think must be thought with our entire being, body and soul.

Desire to be a bird, desire to become a bee. Man feels that his happiness is in the air.—And if we wish to become a bird, it is not an eagle, a vulture, a pheasant, a partridge, or a parrot that we wish to become, but a modest little bird gifted with amiability, a warbler, a titmouse, a robin, a nightingale, an average and innocent bird. For neither do we wish to become a hummingbird.

Always to explain the moral world by the physical world is not necessarily a good idea. For in the physical world we often take appearances for realities and our conjectures for facts. We thus risk making two errors instead of one by applying to one world the false dimensions we give to the other. Applications of the moral world to the political world are more appropriate.

Shadows on the wall: judgments, conjectures.

Everything is double and is made up of a soul and a body. The universe is the body of God (but here the body is in the soul). The mind's body is matter. There is the body of the body. The body of the rarefied is the dense, and the hard is the body of the dense. Always and endlessly, the thick and the thin hold to the inner and the outer. Everything is made of more and less. No body without soul, no soul without body. If there is the body of the body, there is perhaps also the soul of the soul.

Nota. How it happens that in searching for words we come to ideas. Words are the bodies of thoughts.

(For the child.)
Does he speak?—No, he does not speak to us, but he hears us.—Did he make this tree?—No, but he made the first tree, and all the others have come from it.

In heaven there is a great book. Everything we say, do, and think is written in it.—In what language?—God knows, but we do not know. Yes, what we are saying now, what we will say today, and all that we can say for as long as our life lasts.

Can we see him?—We can see him with our mind.—Why not in another way?—Because our eyes prevent it. God does not have a body like ours: that is why we cannot see him when we have a body. He gave us his idea. . . We will know him when we are in heaven. . . A child cannot know what a man knows, a man cannot know what an angel knows, an angel cannot know what God knows.

Sometimes, in order for a thing to be used, what is superfluous is essential. Thus the flesh of a pear is worth more to us than its seeds, even though for its reproduction, which is the great goal of nature, the seed is what is necessary, sufficient unto itself, and the flesh is what is superfluous, too much.

The style is the thought itself.

How, when languages are formed, ease of expression is harmful to the mind, for no obstacle thwarts it, contains it, makes it cautious, or forces it to choose among its thoughts, a choice it is forced to make in languages that are still new, by the delay that requires it to look for its words and to search through its memory. In this case one can write only with great attention.

Every body is no more than a film (I speak of bodies that move and that have a soul within them). All depth is only a point. All weight is the weight of a straw, a particle of feather . . . even less.

J.-J. Rousseau. In his books we learn how to be discontented with everything outside of ourselves.

God. It would not be bad to represent him through perfumes and light, with light at the center.

This life, which holds our soul in the cradle, if I can express myself in this way. It surrounds the mind with swaddling clothes and covers it with obscurities.

Passions. The ancients called them *troubles*; and rightly so: why.

Beyond bodies, beyond worlds, beyond everything,—beyond and around bodies, beyond and around worlds, beyond and around everything, there is light and there is mind. Without mind, I mean the elemental mind, everything would be full and nothing would be penetrable; there would be no movement, no circulation, no life.

When children ask for an explanation, and we give it to them and they do not understand it, they are still satisfied and their minds have been put at rest. And yet what have they learned? They have learned that what they no longer wish not to know is very difficult to know, and in itself this is a kind of knowledge. They wait, they are patient, and with reason.

Memory.—It is a mirror that retains, and retains forever. Nothing is lost in it, nothing is erased. But it can be tarnished. And then one sees nothing in it.

J.-J. Rousseau. Of the power of words. Of their heat. Warm words. This style that makes us feel its flesh and blood.

The memory of death: is it not able to maintain in us the natural compassion we have for suffering?—And this death, this childhood, etc.

Newton. It is no more true that he has discovered the system of the world than it is true that someone who balances the accounts of an administrator has discovered a system of government.

Beautiful clothes are a sign of joy.

The skies of skies, the sky of the sky.

[1799]

Like Daedalus, I am forging myself wings. I construct them little by little, adding one feather each day.

Illusion or play. Everything agreeable is in them.

When men lose their childishness, that readiness of childhood to fear and honor powers that are invisible, when an excessive mental audacity puts them above all belief, then they have left the sphere of the accustomed order, they have passed the limits within which their nature is good, and they become wicked.

The marriage of the soul and the body. . . . Their agreement is delicious, but their disputes are cruel.

To warm himself in the sun of laziness. . .

Passions are only natural. It is the lack of repentance that corrupts.

The evening meal is the joy of the day.

How it happens that only in looking for words do we find thoughts.

We have philosophized badly.

To hear with the eyes, to see with the ears, to represent with air, to circumscribe in a small space great voids and fullnesses. What am I saying? Immensity itself and all matter, such are the incontestable and easily verified marvels that are perpetually at work in speaking and writing.

Hollowed ideas. The beautiful meaning we find in this word when we consider its good part. Hollowed like a palace and not like a cave. Hollowed; you can enter and find marvels there, riches and beauty, greatness and pleasure. Hollowed and transparent like crystal vases made of celestial essences. Hollowed like the cedar columns in which treasures are hidden.

But the voice is not made only of air, but of air modeled by us, impregnated by our heat and enveloped like some kind of skin by the vapor of our inner atmosphere accompanied by some emanation that gives it a certain shape and certain properties capable of producing effects upon other minds.

Heaven will abolish the language in which these works are written.

To foresee with power is to see. What one foresees in this way makes present.

The earth is a point in space, and space is a point in the mind. By mind I understand here the spiritual element, the world's fifth element, the space of everything, the bond of all things, for all things are there, live there, move there, die there, are born there.—Mind. . . the last hold of the world.

There are those to whom one must advise madness.

Souls must not be taken to the brothel.—And: it is perfectly acceptable to go to a brothel, but no one must be taken there.
    Nota. Repentance.

When you want transparency, the finite, the smooth and the beautiful, you must polish for a long time.

Children. Let the child earn his name.

Our mind must not be more difficult than our taste, nor our judgment more severe than our conscience.

What is so finished, so exact in its expression and, in a word, so perfect, has a kind of form so determined and solid that the imagination of the reader has nothing to do and nothing to react to and therefore does not open its memory to appropriate it and retain it. We leave this memory before ourselves, to admire it, but outside of us. We are struck and not penetrated. There is nothing fluid or pithy about it, except perhaps that the thought in itself is so ethereal that it dematerializes the word.

Minds. Exist almost alone. Matter is used only to give them an envelope. It is a simple effigy: its weight and intensity are only an appearance. And nevertheless we speak of mass, of thickness, and of enormous weights. It is because we ourselves are inexpressibly light of matter. A speck of dust in the eye seems as hard as a pebble. It is because our eye is tender. A piece of straw against the pupil is as strong as a beam of wood. A hand in front of our view blocks it like a mountain. It is because the visual orbit is a point of extreme delicacy.

To know how many millions of leagues the earth is from the sun. It is a decidedly useless number to know, for it serves absolutely nothing. But to know how to measure this distance and how it has been measured is not useless. The fact is nothing, but the discovery of it is beautiful. I mean that the industry that led to it is worthy of admiration and can be usefully applied to more important measurements.

Clocks must regulate watches, just as laws must regulate particular actions. But the sun must regulate the clocks and justice must regulate the laws.

Adventurous minds, which wait for and receive their ideas only from chance.

Ink and paper should not be used in the way the air and the voice are used. We must not be forced to listen too long to those who cannot escape us. Some are much more interested in explaining their thought than in making it heard. It is enough, however, to make it heard. Instead of speaking, they compose. This is bad writing. There are, however, occasions when an air of concern, of attention, and even affectation can be suitable. . . .

We use for passions the stuff that has been given to us for happiness.

Of the necessity of reforming ideas in order to reform judgments.

My soul lives in a place where the passions have passed by and where I have known them all.

Lions, bulls; images of strength are everywhere, whereas images of wisdom are nowhere.

He gives his body up to pleasure, but not his soul.

Art is another nature that men have made. I call it nature because it has always been present; wherever there are men, they paint, they sing, they build.

We must treat our lives as we treat our writings, put them in accord, give harmony to the middle, the end, and the beginning. In order to do this we must make many erasures.

Strong and concise style. This must be the end, not the beginning. Refine what is subtle, change the solid into fluid, and the fluid into smoke: stop with the vapor, the cloud, etc.

Children and people with weak minds ask if the story is true.

People with healthy minds want to know if it is moral, if it is naive, if it must be believed.

Dreams of love. Those of ambition. The dreams of piety.

When the image masks the object, when one makes a body out of shadow, when the word debauches the mind in charming it, when the expression pleases so much that we no longer go beyond it to penetrate the meaning, when the figure itself absorbs all our attention, we are stopped on the path. The road has been taken for the dwelling place. A bad guide is leading us.

Let us remember that everything is double.

We must not entrust children with fire, nor the furious with iron.

Arrival of Bonaparte.

They are capable? Yes, but they are not respected.

. . . like regret, which is the salt of absence and image . . .

But in fact what is my art? What is the name that distinguishes this art from others? What end does it propose? What does it produce? What does it give birth to and make exist? What do I pretend to do and what do I want to do in doing it?

Is it writing in general, to assure myself of being read? The one ambition of so many people! Is that all I want? Am I no more than a polymath? Or do I have a class of ideas that is easy to label and whose nature, character, merit, and use can be determined?

This must be examined attentively, at great length, until I know the answer.

Children are well cared for only by their mothers and men only by their wives.

—Of destructive power . . .

Few men, in these great political dramas, are capable of inventing a role, many are capable of playing it.

Old men, when neglected, have no more wisdom.

Plato is the Rabelais of abstractions.

Don't throw your mind into flowing waters.

Kings no longer know how to rule.

[1800]

Uproot? No, but transplant.

How through memory a person is one, and how without it there is no more I, or at least a continuous I, no more past, no more future, nothing but a numerical and mathematical present that is susceptible neither to addition nor division.

The ancients extolled music because (they said) it suppressed passions (at least earthly ones). We praise it because it gives them.

Our eye prevents us from seeing: it is our body that prevents us from touching. Between us and the truth there are our senses, which introduce a part of the truth in us and which also separate us from it. This separation, necessary to the formation of the soul, is sensitive to it, etc.

There emerge from us bright shadows or images, just as there emerge dark shadows or shadows properly speaking.

There is something luminous in the face that is not found in the other parts of the body.

Each man thinks not what he has been told but what he understands.

The word, in fact, is disembodied thought.

Antiquity. I prefer ruins to reconstructions.

That little matter was enough. That in itself it is little. From which the idea of the ancients that there was only one world.

Necessity of matter. That without it God could not have separated anything from himself and that the creation would not have taken place.

That God is being. Meaning of this word, which must be taken in its strictest sense.

It would be difficult to be scorned and to live virtuously. We have need of support.

Children. Need models more than critics.

God is God. Nothing is God but himself.

. . . the whole world.—seems no more to the eyes—than a rainbow.

The hardest matter, the matter we find the darkest, shines for them, and not only with seven colors but with a million. It is for our eyes that all the streams and interplays of light unfold. A diamond lost in the lawn is only a stone for the caterpillar who crawls along it, but for us it is a source of radiant scintillations. It is a star. It is a meteor.

Thus the earth, for example . . . We are . . . Minds are . . .

Of the beauty of matter.

All ardent people have something mad about them, and all cold people have something stupid.

When I say "matter is appearance," I do not pretend to challenge its reality, but, on the contrary, to give a true idea of its real precariousness.

Every stone is a paste that has dried. Every metal is a body in fusion that has cooled and hardened. All matter is tensile, or fusible, or malleable, or all can be divided into invisible and impalpable parts by crushing and pulverization, if the body is solid, and by evaporation if it is already fluid. Marble, lead, can become a cloud, from evaporation to evaporation.

Wood is composed of lines or cores pressed against each other; it is fusible. Stone is made of coagulated dust grains; it is fusible; crystal is a hardened water. Pumice stone is charred: it is the white coal of a stone; it has little water. Water, as the poets say, is a liquid crystal.

Every surface offers a network in which transverse lines cross in every direction. . . .
     A leaf of water, a thinned leaf. . . . A window is a hardened leaf, a leaf of glass. It is a sort of vaporous efflorescence. . .
     Enamel, color . . .

Analysis: in morality, in cooking.

What is closest to our senses and farthest from our soul.

Descartes's noises. His physics has too much commotion. Newton's offers us a more silent world, but too naked, too lifeless.

Of all bodies, fire is the most susceptible to receiving light; but is it luminous in itself?

Numbers exist,—for they exist in our mind,—and it exists.

A knowledge that corks the mind.

Only one grain of matter was needed to create the world. But a whole world was needed to create one soul. It is a work that cannot be done with little.

First, an envelope of celestial matter is needed so that it can be shaped. This envelope must be placed in a thousand others and these thousand others in a body. This body must then be surrounded by air, this air then filled with effluvium by means of water, then, if it is too full, emptied by means of fire, and man then given a pedestal. There must be the earth, there must be the sea, there must be the stars, there must be the world. I have said: "The world is a place."

The more I demean matter to make man stand out, the more I call attention to it and give it dignity.

Descartes must be reproached for his machines but not his ghosts. Too much and not too little materiality ruined his physics and his subtle matter is not subtle enough. He offers things and dust to the imagination rather than air and ether.

We can see in the example provided by Saunderson that in this century one can know optics perfectly without having the slightest idea about vision.

He who has the abstract idea of a thing understands it; but only he who can make it understood is able to make it imaginable. Yes.

Neither pain nor pleasure exists outside our soul, and nevertheless these are realities more important and more real than iron, lead, marble, and all bodies taken together.

Of the world known by the ancients.—That it seemed more in keeping with the range of human intelligence. That this is because they knew better than we do how to envisage all things in a manner appropriate to placing them in their minds. That our minds are still astonished by our new discoveries and that instead of detaching ourselves from this affectation we affect a type of eloquence that continually strengthens it within us. That instead of enlarging our thoughts we enlarge the objects of our thoughts, presenting ourselves with the extraordinary and seeking to astonish our eyes. That instead of raising our minds above the world and all things we raise all things above our minds. That we turn ourselves into dwarfs in order to produce giants and diminish ourselves to make our conceptions more colossal. That the mind must dominate everything and that when it is dominated this means it is in the wrong place.

My vapors stop at my stomach.

Truth consists of having the same idea about something that God has.

Not only are there innate ideas, but *immediate truths*, which we feel, without intervention, without any intermediary.

73

Everything is a game except what makes the soul better
or worse.

There are truths that instruct, perhaps, but they do not
illuminate. In this class are all the truths of reasoning.

The old age of men resembles their childhood. Without
exception.

To breathe pleasure . . .

The least thing put between God and us separates us from him.
Let us overcome it to be one with him.
    Between him and us there must be a veil, but not a wall.

The nightingale . . .

Lively minds and passionate men whose hearts, one might
say, beat too fast.—The effect of a pendulum that swings
too fast.

Echo: *vocis imago*.

In water, in our eyes, in our mirrors. We say that an object "paints itself there." To follow this idea. That vision is made through colors.

Our eyes, water, and mirrors are canvasses for portraits in which objects are represented faithfully through the colors they send out; and not only are the features of objects represented there, but also their mobility in action.

That in the arts, not just painting, but also simple drawing, things exist through colors, as well as in writing. Nothing can be separated and made distinct in our eyes except through two or more colors.

A body paints itself in giving off its colors.

Life enters there, in the same way a lighted candle placed in a lantern also carries light.

We are worth more when someone looks at us. And, because of this, an eye is always watching us.

Let us remember this.—What?—That it is not the sun in the sky that we see, but the sun at the back of our retina.

On Berkeley. To say there are figures without bodies is to pretend there are embroideries without material.

Light. I cannot be satisfied with little.

Shyness and erasures. It is impossible for me to say something foolish without being aware of it.

And then it is not the word that concerns me, it is the thought, which is still not entirely mine, and which I look for uselessly in the sentence. In general, my spirit of good faith rarely runs after words, except to find its thought.

The world and the room; books and the magic lantern.

Solitude gives an *I*.

I that gives solitude. It is in our thoughts, and the one the world gives is in our feelings. Because solitude grows accustomed to seeing, to contemplating; and the world, to acting for itself.

You have searched in vain, you have found nothing but envelopes. Open a hundred, open a thousand, you will always be stopped before opening the last. You think you have touched the essence when you take off the outer skins. You take the homunculus for the animal. But it is much deeper. These worms, these needles, etc., are only . . . The true principle of life, the seed, the essence, the point that holds the animal, etc.

In each drop is a drop, in each point another point.

—The last is a worm; but what is inside the worm?

Nota. In opposition, works of art that have nothing inside them.

Politeness is the art of being bored without boredom or (if you prefer) of bearing boredom without being bored.

Pride swells the brain. Vanity carries with it smoke, minds. Hatred tightens the heart. Love warms the lungs. Admiration stops the heart. We breathe through desire. We want to pump up all that delights, that dilates. Sadness is inaction.

The love that comes from the blood, the love that comes from the soul.

Sneezes of the mind. The palace of sneezes.

Bonaparte in Milan. His speech to the patriots.

Music.—Singing demands another use of the throat and has a different voice character from that of speaking.

Singing is not just fitting words and noises together with a certain exactitude and precision. Singing presents our ears with a voice and accents that move the imagination.

Those who sing well have an echo in their throat and an unidentifiable softness. Those who sing in the way they speak do not sing, but they speak in cadence. Song must be to speech what verse is to prose.

Nothing that is proved is obvious; for what is obvious shows itself and cannot be proved.

God's memory. His imagination.

"The sound must seem an echo to the sense." This expression is from Pope. It is very beautiful.

The mind of every author has its faults. But every author does not show his faults in his works. We pardon those who know how to hide them.

To speak with his imagination, but to think with his reason.

To make oneself ignorant.

I would like thoughts to follow one another in a book like stars in the sky, with order, with harmony, but effortlessly and at intervals, without touching, without mingling; and nevertheless not without finding their place, harmonizing, arranging themselves. Yes, I would like them to move without interfering with one another, in such a way that each could survive independently. No overstrict cohesion; but no incoherence either; the lightest is monstrous.

Let us not confuse what is merely intelligible, that is to say, easily understood, with what is clear.

To make enough space to open his wings.

The poet must not cross an interval with a step when he can cross it with a leap.

Rubens. Concave eye, microscope.

To play with sounds (or words) when the results of this game do not lead to any confusion of meaning, but on the contrary lead to clarity—this game gives pleasure.

Thus, names are correctly applied only when they are *necessary names*, and they are *necessary names* only when no others can signify what they signify,—and, if they do not already exist, they would have to be invented.

Notions that seem to impregnate the mind.

Resemblances. And whether they do not sometimes work through a sort of reflection, which the animated body is capable of imbibing, so to speak, and persistently.—Farmers' wives and their chickens.

The things that we know when not thinking of them.

Where do ideas go?—They go into the memory of God.

Nota. To define light to a blind man, noise to a deaf man, thought to an idiot.

Young people . . . They give their minds much exercise but little food.

Repentance consumes.—And what does it consume?—It consumes the faults and the tendency that caused them.

Ideas never lack for words. It is words that lack ideas. As soon as the idea has come to its last degree of perfection, the word blossoms; or, if you like, it blossoms from the word that presents it and clothes it.

Blind people are cheerful because their minds are not distracted by the representation of things that can please them and because they have even more ideas about spectacles than we do.

If a blind man asked me: "What is light?" I would answer: "What makes us see."—"What is seeing?"—"It is to have an idea of what is before our eyes without having to think about it."

Those mental traits that lead us to hideous obscurities.

Thoughts that cannot survive the test of the open air and that evaporate as soon as we take them out of our room. To put them to the test of isolation. Take them out of the book where you found them: they do not endure.

The air is sonorous, and sound is made of air, of air that is uttered, vibrant, shaped, articulated.

But the idea of the nest in the bird's mind, where does it come from?

An idea can be produced from something or from nothing, and provided this nothing is constant, the idea has no less existence or importance.

That we cannot conceive of the idea of time without the idea of eternity, nor the idea of place without that of space and infinite extension.

When? you say. I answer you:—When I have circumscribed my sphere.

Animate flour. Leavening, in effect, is animation, life, a mind, a soul put into the dough.

It is through the imagination that one is a metaphysician.

On the need for the beautiful,—natural to certain minds and highly developed in others. Defects of style of which it is the cause.

This need for the beautiful creates a habit, almost a necessity, of putting into the expression much art and force when the thought or the subject in themselves have no great merit. With this character and type of mind one cannot write simply or naturally except when one has thoughts that are beautiful. Wait for them.

Of words that take up so much attention that they turn us away from the thought. (Vid. supra.) These shocking, astonishing, striking words are sometimes the only way to make a thought palpable. It can be articulated only through them. They are especially capable (and they alone), they alone are capable of bringing out the attitudes and movements of the mind, operations that are just as agreeable, just as useful, and just as important to know as the thoughts themselves.

To know: it is to see inside oneself.

Perhaps (and probably) it would be true to say that we cannot conceive of anything except what we can see in our minds.

Truth. To surround it with figures and colors, so that it can been seen.

It is very difficult to be wise (through the mind); it is not difficult to be wise occasionally and by chance, but it is difficult to be wise assiduously and by choice.

Everyone makes and has need of making a world other than the one he sees.

Leibnitz and Spinoza.—The realm of abstraction. The first offers its perfection, the second nothing but its flaws.

Condillac. Perception (he says) produces attention. But attention leads to perception. We can therefore consider it as preexistent to perception and in fact it often is. But one would answer that the first perception came before the first act of attention. That matters little, and it will always be true to say that in the formed man who is able to . . . otherwise.

To analyze, to deconstruct.—What they so emphatically call analysis is what we would call division when speaking simply.

The subject must be analyzed in terms of itself, that is, it must be considered from all sides and examined part by part, turned and turned again. Everything must be said concisely and simultaneously after having been examined repeatedly and at length. The writer must be like a painter. The painter considers his model trait by trait, but it is the whole that he shows. It is not ray by ray, but through facets, that the light shines for us.

Phantoms of thoughts! . . .

If prayer does not change our destiny, it changes our feelings—which is no less useful.

How admiration contributes to the peace of the human mind and is necessary to it.

Every house: temple, empire, school.

In our writings thought seems to move like a man who is walking straight ahead. On the other hand, in the writings of the ancients, thought seems to move like a bird that glides and advances by turning round and round.

Everything seems naked to eyes that have never seen without veils. Nothing can please them for very long.

[1801]

History, like perspective, has need of distance.

Close your eyes and you will see.

This man too has need of perspective. You come too close to him with your eye.

Vision is made by the joining of two lights.—Add. March 19: And if objects shine toward us, we shine toward objects.

Minds that are made of material, and so much so they spread only shadow, like bodies that are opaque.

To want to know invariably and fixedly what is only vague, and vaguely what is fixed and solid, is finally to know neither one nor the other.

And what am I but an atom in a ray?

The poet. He paints passions under glass.

Christianity. We cannot speak against it without anger, nor speak for it without love.

Logic is a demi-geometry and metaphysics is a demi-poetry that gives a transparent body to what has no body, just as poetry gives a soul.

Another feature of pure and elementary truth: pleasure; the pleasure the soul receives from it.

Figure, movement. Everything happens, says Pascal, from figure and movement. To say in this case that everything happens from movement, for every figure is no more than the lingering trace of a movement that has already ceased. Thus the letters I am forming now, for example, are only the pen's lingering trace of the movement of my hand.

Objects must be described only in order to describe the feelings they evoke in us.

There grows up between our senses and all our perceptions, between the shocks of all things and all their commotions, between all agitations and our resolve, a distance, an interval, a time, a void, a space where everything becomes calm, tempered, dim, silent, slow.

I have not seen you since, but you have often appeared to me in my dreams.

In those days they took allusions from the world and today we are forced to take them from books. This is a disadvantage.

Yes, we have three eyes, we also have three ears (as the Chinese author said). For in addition to the two eyes and two ears of the body, we must also consider the ear of the soul, the invisible eye of the mind.

    The imagination is an eye where images remain forever.

At ten o'clock this evening. My poor mother! My poor mother!

"To bury your life" is lovely. (Volt. Irèn.)

It is the bell that moves, but you who ring. It is the sun that shines, but you who see. The nourishment is in the meat, but the taste is in you. Fire gives or creates warmth, but it is you who feel it.

    Harmony is in the one who listens: yes, as effect; but not as cause.

I like Leibnitz's expression *the soul carries the body*. And observe that everywhere and in everything, what is subtle carries what is compact; and what is light holds in suspension all that is heavy. Admit it, at least in the sense of——and as the most beautiful conception of the human mind.

This stone in my hand, it demands glory.

Somber and unhappy lovers of a murderous equality.

I thus call space everything that is not myself, that is not determined.

In the places where I live. I always want much sky to be mixed with little earth; this can only be done when. . .

And what do the diverse pleasures roused in us by books, paintings, conversations, etc., consist of, if not that they show us (more or less) the nakedness of thoughts, ideas, minds, souls more or less whole, perfect, complete? And what pleases you in the fortuitous arrangements or orderings of raw nature, if not that they more or less resemble a thought, a drawing, drawings or thoughts that please us, and all the more so because they are not rigorously determined, which gives us the advantage of conceiving of them in the way we like best?

A thought is a thing as real as a cannon ball.

One must write with effort in centuries of bad taste.—Why?—
Facility would reinforce the reader's weariness. How?

To seek the truth. But, as you are seeking and as you are waiting,
what will you do, what will you think, what will you practice,
what rules must you follow?

The spectacle has changed, but our eyes are the same.

No, I am not angry with myself, but I am angry with books.

This young man you call Bonaparte . . .

Everything beautiful is indeterminate.

To use reason to give us passions.—Monstrosities.—No . . .—How.

It is an opera without orchestra, a song without accompaniment.
It demands an airy style that does not touch the ground.

Do not choose for your wife any woman you would not choose
as your friend if she were a man.

Accountable for their deeds—But, for me—it is my thoughts I account for.

Religion adheres powerfully to the dead.

Beautiful works. Genius begins them, but labor alone finishes them.

Of the unfortunate need to please oneself.

Newton. How ripe his apple was.

Banish from words everything equivocal, everything indeterminate; make them, as they say, into invariable numbers: if there is no more play in the word, from then on there is no more eloquence or poetry; all that is mobile and variable in the soul's affections would remain without possible expression. But what did I say, banish . . . I say more. If you banished all abuse from words, there would not even be any axioms. (Vid. d'Alembert, Discourse on the Encyclopedia.) It is the equivocality, the uncertainty, that is to say, the suppleness of words that is one of their great advantages for creating an exact usage.

Faculty of inventing languages—is an industry natural to our intelligence.

In the end, God loves each man as much as he loves mankind. Weight and number are as nothing in his eyes. Eternal, immense, infinite, he has only immense loves.

Expiate dreams.

How it is always through the beyond and not through the within that all languages become corrupted. Through the beyond of their usual sound, their natural energy, their habitual force, etc. It is fracas that accompanies their decadence and luxury that corrupts them.

We are all old children, more or less serious, more or less filled with ourselves.

We still know how to mark the hours, but no longer how to ring them. The carillon of our clocks is missing.

It seems more difficult to me to be a modern than to be an ancient.

[1802]

Floods of passions. It would nevertheless be better to raise the dikes for them.

That God has the idea of our ideas. Now, if God has the idea of our ideas, it follows that, etc.

A presumption in favor of the resemblance of our ideas with the object. Our identity with God? But who would dare to speak in this way? Let us simply say therefore: our participation in the divine intelligence.

From this day forward, to give up Locke, and to agree never to read another word he has written.

What will you think of pleasures when you no longer enjoy them?

The only thing Newton invented was the how much.

The things we believe are difficult to conceive of because it is difficult to talk about them.

In fact everything (according to Descartes) everything happens through figure and movement. That is the fixed point from which his mind proceeded to all its operations, the result of his explanations. That is his doctrine, summed up in a few words. Goodbye, Descartes!

The white markings of the snow, here and there, scattered on the greenness in time of thaw.

The shadow of smoke, in the sunlight. —Jan. 21: in the ice.

All beings come from little, and little is needed for them to come to nothing.

You say that books are soon read, but they are not soon understood. To digest them, etc. To understand a beautiful or great thought perhaps requires the same amount of time it takes to have it, to conceive of it. To penetrate a thought and to produce a thought are almost the same action.

Piety is a cure.

Dream. Lost memory.

We can say of all poems that are not born as if from themselves and delivered (if we can speak this way) from the heart and womb of revery: these are poems that do not have a mother— *prolem sine matre cretam*. They all have something imperfect about them, something unfinished.

Lafontaine. The expression in his verse is imperfect, undecided. But the poet's disposition is very marked and the work pleases because of that. This shows that the highly pronounced attitude of a man who dreams is pleasant to us, even if we don't know what he's dreaming about.

When I glow . . . I lose my oil.

In our efforts to remember, we are searching.—Where are we searching? Where? In our idea,—in the canvas, in the mirror, in the atmosphere that is between our senses and our mind.

We are in life more to act than to know. But to realize even this, that we are in life, etc., we must know. And even this is a kind of acting, knowing. It is one of our duties.

One would say that in such dark eyes there is a flame without light.

Imagined harmonies. If they are not a physical fact, they are at least a human fact, and because of that, a reality.

If a superior intelligence wanted to give an account of human things to the inhabitants of heaven and to give an exact idea of them, he would express himself like Homer.

I pass my life chasing after butterflies—considering the ideas
that conform to generally held ideas as good, and the others
simply as mine.

. . . and the minds that are sympathetic to my own.

Balance. We look for it in order to go to sleep. If interior, easy to
find. If not, difficult. —So little needed to establish it: the folding
or unfolding of a sheet is enough.

Scrupulous taste. Scrupulous people rarely do great things.

That is true, a king without religion always seems a tyrant.

The revolution chased my mind from the real world by making
the world too horrible for me.

Those ideas that dispose the mind to produce the truth.

In morality (a science of practice and circumstances) the individual
is made for society. But in metaphysics (and even in religion),
a science of real essences, society is made for individuals.

It is even easier to be wrong about truth than about beauty.

In order for a style to be considered good, it must, so to speak, detach itself from the paper, in the same way that the colors and figures detach themselves from a good painting.

Men do not want to learn unfashionable truths except when they are spared the pains of attention.

It seems that Plato has too much and that there is too little in Aristotle. From which, in the first, an abundance carried to superfluity, and in the other a precision or brevity that leads to obscurity.

Speak more softly to be better heard by a deaf public.

To call everything by its name.

Illusas que auro vestes (Virg.) Magic is needed everywhere. It exists in painting through color, in sculpture through [   ] and in music through tone, which creates the effect of speaking without words. Even a beautiful fabric has magic: silk, a fine sheet, velvet, and even what they call "fine whites."

Illusion based on reality, that is the secret of the fine arts—in fact, of all art.

We speak to ourselves in metaphors. We are naturally led to it as a method of better understanding ourselves and of retaining our thoughts more easily—which we then label in a kind of container.

"In a container of light." Y.

Metaphysics. A vast science in which everything is true, even what is contradictory, as in a vast countryside the same towers are both round and square.

There are only two kinds of beautiful writing, that which has a great fullness of sound, meaning, soul, warmth, and life, and that which has a great transparency.

We have it in our soul, but we hardly ever put into our life what we put into our writings.

If I weigh myself down, everything is lost.

In every piece of music, not everything is music, and in every poem not everything is poetry.

Fear feeds the imagination.

Happy people strike me as children; people who are too serious and especially those who are proud strike me as dwarfs. Or rather, those who are vain strike me as children; those who are prideful strike me as dwarfs.—Children and dwarfs. Their difference: a dwarf is the size of a child, but with a man's face.

The first act of a man who finds God displeasing is to say to himself: I must arrange the world without him.

Imagining is good, provided you do not believe you see what can only be imagined.

Lost spirit. Judges without justice, priests without religion.

Sensibility that comes from the nerves. Opinions have a great influence on it and can lead to cruelty. Examples in the revolution.

(At the baths.) Piety defends us from ourselves; modesty defends us from others.

(5 in the morning. Insomnia.) Everything must have its sky. To be put everywhere.

There are many situations in life that we suddenly feel we
have seen in dreams.

The sky or perspective is what makes poetry. The echo is what
makes music. The bright and the dark in painting. The dreamed,
or the hollow of the brain, in all things. The soul, finally, or the
mind and the spiritual world, etc. Space.

Tragic actors. Express sensation more than sentiment.

Fixed style.—Of a man who has dreamed a great deal with
himself, or of a man who has arranged in advance the style
he will write in. Between these two *fixed styles* there is a great
difference. The second is mere labor, a mechanism of professional
work. The other is a true operation of the mind. And it is
natural; reflection is as natural as flowing water.

All beautiful words are susceptible to more than one meaning
(or signification).

Every excess is a mistake.

The phrase: "One dies because one has lived."

Two things can never be the object of the same thought at the same time unless there is some symmetry *uniting* them or turning the two things into a single thing.

Symmetry. Or correspondence. Secret link, etc. Through it a middle is created (at the point of contact), a middle, I say, from which one can perceive the extremities.

My memory holds no more than the essence of what I read, of what I see and even of what I think.

The breast. This new ornament makes those who have it and are not used to it blush.

Those minds in which there is always something beyond their thought and, so to speak, that do not have limits.

To truth by way of illusion.

Sad science that teaches blind men to speak of light and colors and that persuades them they can even make judgments about these things.

A heart of beef is not a heart. (MmeJ.)

The child speaks words with his memory long before he speaks them with his tongue.

[1803]

Nothing is more difficult for children than reflection. That is because the last and essential destination of the soul is seeing, is knowing, and not reflecting. Reflection is one of the labors of life, a means of getting somewhere, a path, a passage, and not a center. Everything always tends towards its final destination. To know and be known, these are the two points of rest. This will be the happiness of souls.

The weather strikes me on the head. I feel it rattle my teeth.

. . . but in the end a year comes when you find that you are getting old.

To treat these materials well (metaphysical subjects), we must get as far away from the philosophers and as close to the poets as we can.

Stacking the dead on top of each other.

Those heavy minds that annoy us with their weight and

immobility. You can't make them fly or swim. Because they don't know how to help themselves, they grab hold of you and drag you down.

Minds that love to wheel around like birds, to rise up, to glide, to wander, to cleave the air in order to come back to a fixed point, a solid and precise point.

To know how to walk in the night, to have a goal, to reach it in the darkness, the shadows.

That the history of our thoughts (in spite of us and without our knowledge) is found in our language. This notion of G.'s is very good, very right, and the idea is very true.—Observation: G. never said this. I was wrong. He simply said that language in general should be considered a monument to human reason.

Everything is made through images. They enter us through all the other senses, as through the eye. An echo (they say) is an image of the voice. All our affections are produced by images of touching. Our whole body is a mirror.

Pleasures that we can perceive only when they no longer give us pleasure.

Someone said of an asthmatic who was being very sweet and patient in his suffering: "One would like to breathe for him."

The natural pace of the mind. And how it should move so as not to get worn out by quickness or bogged down and made impatient by slowness.

Disagreeable shortcuts of style.

Fleeting irrelevancies often serve to stamp solid objects in our memory; a sound, a song, an accent, a voice, a smell engrave forever in our mind the memory of certain places, because these small things were what made up our pleasure or boredom there.

Yes. Whether thought can exist outside the mind in the same way a word can exist outside the mouth.

Turning round in my mind for a long time.
    Not to write, at such moments, with one's resources.
    To gather my earth. First of all, it must be left to stand. Later, there will be nothing left to do but grind it up.
    To make work easier.

The same feature that is agreeable when it is fleeting becomes hideous when it remains fixed. That is because mobility is the essence of what is agreeable.

Everything must be precise in it and yet nothing should be too tight.

Let the work be complete and round.

In fact the word is the sign of a thought and writing is the sign of the word. That is to say, it is only the sign of another sign.

. . . because, what must be put in the work and what must be left out is infinite.

For the first form and idea of a work must be a space, a simple place where the material can be put, arranged, not a material to be put somewhere and arranged.

Debts shorten life.

Minds incapable of care. And: thoughts that have stayed in the mind for a long time. "I lived with the rose." And that: the same taste that leads us to do something well forces us to redo it, to do little, to do slowly, making it difficult for us to approve of what we have done. And that: the best is the enemy of the good only when we look for it and not when we see it. Even more, we do not do well except when we know where the best is and when we are assured that we have touched it and hold its power within us. And that: it is not things that please, but the impression the mind makes on itself, that it puts into itself and leaves there, for only the mind pleases the mind, only the soul pleases the soul. Except one single thing, whose power the mind takes little part in and is independent of thought and will, being necessary to the multiplication of souls and the survival of the human race.

The thoughts that come to us are worth more than the ones we seek.

To know what one must forbid oneself.

Flowers in cemeteries. They must be uprooted; this earth spoils them.—And let the skeletons smile. Horrible amusements.

Chateaubriand. We inhabit the same regions but we do not bring back the same curiosities.

Collections, thoughts. The man shows himself in them, if the author does not.

I have many forms for ideas, but not enough forms for phrases.

My lynx eyes.

I feel the almond in the shell, the water in the earth, the fire in the stone.

To have an attention so firm that it sees ideas as if they were things, and in the same way eyes see the realities before them, in the same way they are painted on the retina.

What we write with difficulty is written with more care, engraves itself more deeply.

. . . this poetry of thought.

. . . and withdraw into that freedom of mind whose charms are dangerous, according to them—but when treated correctly it is certainly the most useful thing in the world.

All nightingales do not sing equally well, nor do all roses smell the same.

Music has seven letters, writing has twenty-six notes.

Rigorously to avoid encountering the limits of your mind.

Widowhood rejuvenates them.

Words like so many tiny wheels.

Lightning flashes that cross the mind and illuminate so quickly
they are hardly noticed. In such cases, more is seen than retained.
Thus, whoever does not observe himself carries within him some
experience he does not know about.

In us there is a corner where we are always young and almost
children. This is not because our thoughts lack meaning
or gravity, but because we are not destined in life for any
serious role.

To live with oneself, that is to say . . .
    "To live medicinally" is not always to live unhappily, no matter
what the proverb says, if during this time one lives with oneself.
    Not how long he has lived, but how long he has lived with
himself and in himself.

In oneself is to have no movements other than those that come from us or from our consent. And with oneself is to feel nothing that is not known to us. It is to be the witness, the confidant, the arbitrator of all that one does and all that one says and all that one thinks. It is at once to live life and to contemplate it. It is to live known by oneself. It is to serve as one's own companion, friend, advisor. It is to age, it is . . .

Anger. Its fermentation is necessary to the maturing of certain soft and peaceful feelings. But if the crisis does not take place, if the fermentation leads only to its own bitterness, the operation has not borne fruit and the natural course of things has not been followed.

It is difficult for me to leave Paris because I must separate myself from my friends; and difficult for me to leave the country because I must separate myself from myself.

. . . speaking only of the head. Voice of the head, mind of the head, opinions of the head.

Words, and whether they are more important than sentences.

The silence of the pen and its advantages. Force builds up in it. Precision must flow out of it. A chatterer fallen quiet. When silence comes from force, it should make itself felt in discourse.

What is hasty would be bad upon reflection.—To know how not to write—to be capable of not writing.

Everything has its poetry.

And those for whom a long old age has seemed to purify the body.

For an expression to be beautiful it must say more than is necessary while nevertheless saying precisely what it must. The *too much* and the *enough* must be united, there must be abundance and economy. The narrow and the wide, the little and the much, must be mingled. The sound must be brief and the meaning infinite. Example: *discentem credere opportet* (Aristot.). Everything luminous has this character. A lamp and its wick perfectly brighten not only the object for which they are used but twenty others for which one did not think of using them.

To write, not only with few words, but with few thoughts.

It would be quite possible to dance or mime one of Sterne's chapters. Even several of Montesquieu's chapters. The chapter on despotism, for example.

The voice is an aid to intelligence.

The soul. It can raise up the body.

Luckily, I never feel at one time more than half my pains.

Two sorts of truths: i. what must be thought, ii. what must be done.

They speak to the ear, I want to speak to the memory.

Yes, a flame without smoke, a light without vapors, that is what I want, but that is what is impossible to have often and even less so always.

Of certain beauties, certain thoughts, certain feelings, certain imaginative traits that are absolutely new. No one was expecting them. Their novelty makes people indecisive. We are afraid to hazard our judgment, to compromise the honor of our opinion. We decide to approve of these things late. We dare not taste them; we want proofs to be provided first. We are completely surprised that these things continue to charm us long after we have seen them for the first time.

Natural! natural! yes, no doubt, natural; but what do they mean by this word? Are the sounds of a flute natural, if by this word we understand a thing that only nature makes?

Finally, when you can't find the word you were looking for, you put down the word that was there, which might lead you to it without your knowing how. This is in fact natural, for nature carries you to it.

Yes, you; because you write with ink. But I write with colors.

And everything comes from the entrails, everything, even the least expression. This is perhaps inconvenient, but necessary: I submit to it.

Attention is sustained (in poetry) by the amusement of the ear. Prose does not have this advantage. Might it have? I try. But I think not.

As the sea touches the moon through its vapors, and the sun, through the length of its rays, touches the earth—distances.

[1804]

Then there comes into languages a facility and an overabundance that, if you want to become a great writer, you must oppose with difficulties, with a sure taste, a meditated choice. When you find a torrent, obstacles must be placed in it.

Strength in organization and weakness in carrying out the material. Like an automaton whose elasticity would be exquisite if the wood were not too thin or too fragile.

There I am: a flattering self-portrait.

To survive one's passions and not one's strengths. Happy.

A poetic vapor, a cloud, that is resolved in prose.

This wisdom. It is constant, but mobile.

Those useless phrases that come into the head. The mind is grinding its colors.

Severe taste and prodigious imagination.

It is beautiful enough to be seen, but not to be dreamed.

God. There are many things that should be left in life and not put into books.

The germinating grass that stirs the earth and leaves around its root the traces of this movement. See the fields.

Memory and rhythm.

It is a key; what difference if it is gold or iron? It can open things.

I have to grind my sentences; and that is the most difficult thing.

Not only the grinding of sentences, but grouping them; and to detach masses from one another: another difficult operation.

And note how in each true meditation a moment of rest follows each movement.

The drop of dew and the diamond: colors and dew play in one and in the other.
    —Like those dark clouds I saw embroidered with light.

When the author speaks to himself instead of speaking to the reader.

Everything that is exact is short.

I am not at the end.

"But he doesn't finish his sentences," (he said). And they don't finish their thoughts.—To finish their thoughts.—To finish one's thought! It is a long process, it is rare. It gives intense pleasure. Because every finished thought easily enters the mind. They don't have the same need to be beautiful in order to please. It is enough for them to be finished. The situation of the soul that has had such thoughts communicates itself to other souls and transfers its repose to them.

Another rain and another clear sky than the rain and clear sky of other men.

The body. Like a piece of clothing that wears out.

These thoughts form not only the foundation of my work, but of my life.

To paint and adorn ideas. Advantages, inconveniences.

Fever. In the swamps of reason.

It is not mental repose they seek, but mental laziness.

Enter oneself (we say). When one enters oneself, one sees God.

God. All other beings are distinguished by their shadow, but he is distinguished by his light.

Lumine vestit. We are all and always clothed with God and invested with his light. We can however not think about it, in the same way we can not think about ourselves.

The finger and the eye of the worker continually placed on his work.

Descartes. His imaginary world is not an imaginable world. In it the mind finds matter everywhere, and figures rather than form. (For the form is the figure of the figure, the figure is the body of the form, the form is the exterior soul of a body.) Descartes has thus made the imagination do what it does not like to do. He has made it arrange stones. It wants to be an architect: he has restricted it to being a mason.

Infinity! We have the sight of it more than the idea.

The heart must walk ahead of the mind, and indulgence ahead of the truth.

I wanted to bypass words, I disdained them: words have had their revenge—through difficulty, etc.

To the question: is he guilty? must be added another question: is he incorrigible?

They want to shake up the world, not make it wiser.

"Life," (I said), "is not given to us to be known, but as a means." B[onaparte] treats men this way. He does not think of knowing them and judging them, but of using them.

The time I once lost in pleasure I now lose in suffering.

When you write easily, you always think you have more talent than you really do.

The anecdote told today by D'Arnaud. "Where did you go, young ladies?"—"We went to see the guillotine, mama; oh dear, how horrible it was for the executioner." This grotesque displacement of pity that shows the true spirit of this century, a century in which everything has been turned upside down.

There is nothing serious in civil life except good and evil, vice and virtue. Everything else in it should be a game.

They are all false, you say? And I say: they are all true.

And perhaps we speak so well only when we don't know exactly what we are going to say.

It is not my words that I polish, but my ideas.

Minds that are eagles, without feathers, without wings.

Of those who feel God as light and of those who feel him as rules.

Of those who feel God as rules, as light, and of those who feel him as love.

Waves of light and layers of brightness.

In the same way crimes have increased laws, errors have increased explanations.

In the way a beam of light pierces a cloud, the light a fog. Or—in the way a movement can penetrate a whole mass without making any change in it.

For the subject must please, and all subjects are difficult.

Children are severe. Why.

Of those who remember their childhood and those who only remember school.

Until the drop of light I need, that I am waiting for, forms and falls.

[1805]

Those thoughts that come to us suddenly and that are not yet ours.

I know too well what I am going to say. I know it too well before writing.

We must try, as much as possible, not to mistrust anyone.

And for this reason our words have too much strength and our thoughts not enough.
  This moderation which makes one robust . . .
  Like those men who say cold things with warmth and weak things with strength, they have teeth and lungs, but not good reasons.

Thoughts that are light, clear, distinct, finished; and words that resemble their thoughts.

Words that often retain their meaning even when they are detached from the others and that please when isolated as sounds.

For simple light is perhaps still more beautiful than colors.

Glory. Lovelier to desire than to possess.

Opinions are things that illuminate—true meteors.

There are words and beauties born from the pen. But . . .

All things that are easy to say have already been perfectly said.

Once we have tasted the juice of words, the mind can no longer pass them by. We drink thought from them.

. . . and, since heaven willed it, to pass my life supporting the weight of my stomach.

Art has nothing to do with such books. They should be left to commerce.

——We at least could have answered him by saying that the sciences are a thing without which we could not have known that the sciences are useless.

And in fact when we remember a beautiful line, a beautiful word, a beautiful phrase, it is always in the air that we read them; we see them before us, our eyes seem to read the words in space. We do not imagine them on the paper where they were written. On the other hand, a vulgar passage does not separate itself from the book where we read it; and it is there that the memory sees it when it is quoted. I say this from experience.

To dominate force. An iron style.

But if we divide what is simple, if we want to divide what is one, if we distribute into several parts what has no joints, we destroy it, we make it immediately unknowable. We have axed it, destroyed it, and still we think it has been analyzed.

I call imagination the faculty of making palpable all that belongs to the mind, of incorporating what is spirit, and, in a word, of unveiling what is invisible to itself without robbing it of its nature.

If, during sleep, God speaks to the soul, we do not know it.

"The art is in hiding art." Yes, in everything that should resemble nature. But isn't there anything that should resemble art and therefore show itself?

My ideas! It is the house for lodging them that costs me so much to build.

In the writings of J.-J. Rousseau for example, the soul is always mingled with the body and cannot be separated from it.

. . . passing their life in contradicting their childhood,—in erasing it.

To live without a body!

Heaven has given children a great abundance of tears.

Architecture of words. (Add): where everything is made with words that can hold themselves in the air. Add again: like sounds. And look for what might give sounds this quality, or what properly constitutes a sound and makes a noise what it is.

. . . with that laughter that seems to rejoice in evil.

————like those acts of justice that corrupt those who commit them.

All these young minds the revolution has heated up and brought to flower before their time, before their age.

To judge things of taste, we must give ourselves time to taste them.

Let us look to beautiful poetry for the material of a beautiful prose.

An oratorical style often has the same drawbacks as those operas in which the music prevents you from hearing the words. Here the words prevent you from seeing the thoughts.

All these writings of which nothing remains, like a stream (clear water rolling over small stones), but the memory of words that have fled.

All reflection is art.

This poetic nudity within words.

The mind. It loves to produce flowers.

And, in fact, when we speak, we write what we are saying in the air.

One can advance a long time in life without aging.

In simple masonry, there are no ideas; in architecture there are. There is a conception from the soul. . . . There is beauty wed to utility. In simple masonry, there is only utility. It houses man as a thing, as an animal, and not as an intelligence. It is concerned with the night and storms more than with the day and peaceful weather.

But a bird's nest, a beaver's house? God had the idea for these things and gave the animal the industry to carry out his thought.

. . . and the delights of the earth. There must be others. . . .

The soul speaks to itself in parables.

All grace (*decor*) comes from patience. And, consequently, from some force exerted on itself.

Like those dreams that have pleased us. They escape us and we vainly try to hold onto them.

My dreams are more amorous than my actions have ever been.

Genius is the aptitude for seeing invisible things, for stirring intangible things, for painting things that have no features.

The human mind. It is a subtle thing and loves subtleties.—All causes are subtle and the effects alone are palpable.

In effect, if we knew perfectly what was happening in heaven, we would be more free of it. And if we knew perfectly what existed on earth, perhaps we would no longer be mortal.

Conversation.—Because they have many of those ideas that, to be shown, have need of eyes, gestures, voice, a whole multitude of signs that the written word does not accompany.
    One sees the soul in operation.

To see the world means judging the judges.

The more I think about it, the more I see that the mind is something outside the soul, just as hands are outside the body, eyes outside the head, branches outside the trunk. It helps to *do*, but not *be* more.

It is not simply a matter of distinguishing between good and evil, but also of not confusing what is laughable with what is not. To make laughable what is not is in some way to make bad what was good.

We are afraid of having and showing a small mind and we are not afraid of having and showing a small heart.

One ruins the mind with too much writing.—One rusts it by not writing at all.

. . . like children's hair, which is always a color that will change.

The little cat and the piece of paper he turns into a mouse. He touches it lightly, for fear of unmasking his illusion.

All ways of expressing ourselves are good if they make us understood. Thus, if the clarity of our thoughts comes through better in a play of words, then the wordplay is good.

One must know how to enter the ideas of others and how to leave them. One must know how to leave one's own ideas and how to come back to them.

They say that souls have no sex; of course they do.

——bodies avid for a new flesh.

Their heads are too small for the greatness of their ideas.

The tulip is a flower without soul, but it seems that the rose and
the lily have one. (The first is beautiful like a young girl.) The rose
is a flower of flesh, the tulip is a flower of cloth, of taffeta. The
lily is beautiful like a young man and we know to what beauties
the rose is often compared. The tulip is a kind of wallpaper.

It seems that there is something spiritual in wine.

In every kind of debauch there enters much coldness of soul. It is
a conscious and voluntary abuse of pleasure.

In everything mathematical there is something imperishable,
because there is nothing living.

I resemble a poplar. This tree always seems young, even when
it is old.

A drop of light is worth more than an ocean of darkness: is worth more, I say, be it given or received.

What man knows only through feeling can be explained only through enthusiasm.

Does God want us to love his enemies?—Yes. Why?

1. A better language has better opinions.—And all my stars in a sky.—All space is my canvas.
11. Stars fall to me from the mind.

It is above all the language for expressing these truths that has not yet been found.

Terrestrial by birth, celestial by origin, only our body is of this world.

Children are people.

There is no metaphysics without the ravishing of the mind, just as there is no poetry without enthusiasm.

A person who is never duped cannot be a friend.

[1806]

I don't like to write anything down on paper that I would not say to myself.

They cling to the gates and see only through the bars.

The important business of man is life, and the important business of life is death.

To descend into ourselves, we must first lift ourselves up.

Deprived for a long time of ideas that suited my mind or of a language that suited my ideas.

One must be an *illusionary* rather than a *visionary*.

Illusions come from heaven and mistakes come from us.

Tacitus. And all those words that are obscure only once.

Before using a beautiful word, make a place for it. Air is needed in front of a facade. An entablature placed in the middle of a wall indicates destruction rather than construction.

... and that I hatch my little eggs, my bird's nest; for my thoughts and my words have wings.

——in these times when, to express ourselves well, we must speak in a way the others do not.

——think nothing outside their paper.

I did not have good eyes nor light in my mind that day.

Marble is concentrated air. I would call the diamond condensed light. The world is a swollen point.

The little girl who hears music for the first time and cries out: "It's God speaking to us!" (In that bad novel by Mme de Genlis.)

Available. A thought is perfect only when it is perfectly available, that is to say when one can place it and detach it at will.

All those for whom style is not a game but a labor.

. . . burdened with the unbearable weight of ourselves.

Facility is the enemy of great things.

Metaphysics. At least the mind finds space in it. Elsewhere it finds only fullness.

All clear and transparent words appear to be beautiful sounds.
    Yes and *no* are not precisely clear words, but definite words. In clear words, there is more light than movement or attitude. *Yes* and *no* are what the Latins called *gestuosa verba*.

Of what is spiritual in matter.

History. We want to find moral lessons in it, but its only lessons are of politics, military art, etc.

What you call weakness comes from the strength of friendship.

Racine is the Virgil of the ignorant.

Beyond the brain, there is something that observes the brain itself.

His hope to "change color."

Undoubtedly, philosophy caused the Revolution. But what caused philosophy? Theological arrogance.

Those who never back down love themselves more than they love the truth.

The music and painting of the streets. Their importance.

Ordinary brightness is no longer enough for me—when the meaning of words is not as clear as their sound—that is, when they do not offer to my thought objects as transparent in themselves as the terms that name them.

From the center we should perceive the circle.

One always adds a little of one's soul to what one thinks.

All gardeners live in beautiful places because they make them so.

Answer:—Those with whom one is happy without saying anything to them.

I have too much brain for my head. It cannot play comfortably in its box.

There must be several voices together in one voice for it to be beautiful. And several meanings in one word for it to be beautiful.

For in spite of ourselves we respect those whom we see respected.

It is through the flesh that we judge what is hard and what is soft.

Man loves what is small; and he loves what is big, through the same weakness.

If, when a stone falls, God helps it to fall.

That man has donkey's ears that don't show.

I have to oil my brain.

I stop when I see no more light; it is impossible for me to write by feeling my way.

——for wine is a wet fire.

[1807]

. . . all the pleasures it does not bless (religion).

Dream of the constellations that withdraw from the sky and set one after the other at sunrise. Beauty of the weather. Magnificence of this spectacle. Among the constellations, some set in the south and others in the north.

Why in language and in the course of all violent passions there is always something familiar and naive.

What is promised to you in dreams is given to you in dreams!

To translate well, art is needed, and much art.

Those who have judgment use it as much in judging stones as in judging men.

Beauty is something animal, the beautiful is something celestial.

To give color and shape to what is diaphanous, and always to give some transparence to what is opaque.—Transparent surfaces.

Thoughts still in seed: they must be left to develop. If we touch them, they will be spoiled.

When what we say is similar to what we are.

In living, one learns how to read. (How, and with what result.)

Little people have few passions, they hardly have anything but needs.

Chinese. This people dressed in silk.

The worker must have his hand on the work,—the thought must survive outside the mind,—and the words must clearly detach themselves from the paper.
     The worker must have his hand on the work: which means that he does not have to rely on explanations, notes, prefaces, etc. The thought must survive outside the mind: which means outside any systems or intentions of the author. And the words

must clearly detach themselves from the paper: which means that they can attach themselves easily to the reader's attention, his memory, that they be suitable for quotation, displacement. . . .

A woman without a belly, a mind without entrails, a mummy who is alive and who moves.

Speak for the ear and write for the memory.

Small books are more durable than big ones; they go farther. The booksellers revere big books; readers like small ones. An exquisite thing is worth more than a huge thing.

A book that reveals a mind is worth more than one that only reveals its subject.

——Like those clocks that ring the same hour twice.

Poetry of ideas.

Winter is more a time of piety. Religious holidays must therefore be more numerous then.

Every composition has need of some repetition in its parts to be well understood and retained by the memory and to strike us as a whole. In all symmetry, there is a middle. Every middle is the knot of a repetition, that is to say, of two similar extremities.

Few minds are spacious; few even have an empty place in them or can offer some vacant point. Almost all have narrow capacities and are filled by some knowledge that blocks them up. What a torture to talk to filled heads, that allow nothing from the outside to enter them! A good mind, in order to enjoy itself and allow itself to enjoy others, always keeps itself larger than its own thoughts. And in order to do this, these thoughts must be given a pliant form, must be easily folded and unfolded, so that they are capable, finally, of maintaining a natural flexibility.

All those short-sighted minds see clearly within their little ideas and see nothing in those of others; they are like those bad eyes that see from close range what is obscure and cannot perceive what is clear from afar. Night minds, minds of darkness.

Great minds are those that disguise their limits, that mask their mediocrity.

During our youth, there is often something in us that is better than ourselves, I mean better than our desires, our pleasures, our yieldings, and our inclinations. Our soul is good then, even though our intelligence and will are not.

Painters say there are pictures in which there is no air. We also have poems with characters in which nothing is located, in which there is no space.

It is impossible to sing and dance correctly without pleasure, since the act of following all true measure is naturally agreeable. But the moral order also consists of measure and harmony, and it is equally impossible to live well without a very great secret pleasure.

It seems to me in fact that our good qualities are more *ourselves* than our faults. Whenever N is not good, it is because he is different from himself.

Whoever does not see his friends in a good light loves them little.
    To see in a good light.—Whoever does not see in a good light is a bad painter, a bad friend, a bad lover. Whoever does not see in a good light has not been able to lift his mind up to what is there or his heart to what is good.

Strength is not energy. Some writers have more muscles than talent.

But if you paint a false window, at least paint it closed. Your lie will be more sensible, will be smaller and will fool people better.
    A stupid lie is one that can never make itself believed.

Someone said (I read it this morning): "Happiness is a hermit." This would not have been said a hundred years ago. At that time one thought (to speak like Chateaubriand) that solitude was good only with God.

People of intelligence often treat business in the way ignorant people treat books: they understand nothing.

In language there are little words that no one has the slightest idea what to do with. M. de Fz uses them with great dexterity.

The first poets or writers made madmen wise. The last seek to make wise men mad.

No, men are not born to know, but they are destined for it.

It is not through the head that men touch each other.

Excess and the *too much* are not the same thing. Excess is worthless, the *too much* is often necessary.

Of those who want us to be wrong and those who want us to be right.

This line (the line of beauty) must unfold without breaking in our head, but it is not possible for the hand to trace it without interruption and without stopping and starting several times.

To want to express such subtle ideas faithfully is to want to capture an object that endlessly escapes and reappears, that shows itself only for a moment. You must wait, in spite of yourself, you must look.

When the last word is always the one that offers itself first, the work becomes difficult.

Heaven gave strength to my mind only for a time—and this time has passed.

All religions = all women.

Properly speaking, man inhabits only his head and his heart. All other places are vainly before his eyes, at his sides, and under his feet: he himself is not there at all.

Those for whom the world is not enough: saints, conquerors, poets, and all lovers of books.

A nail, to hang his thoughts on.

If you want property to be sacred, bring heaven into it. Nothing is sacred where God is not.

A dark point in his mind is as unbearable to him as a grain of sand in his eye.

[1808]

I am like Montaigne: "unsuited to continuous discourse."

Wicked people have nothing human about them except passions: they are almost their virtues.

There is in us a base of joy and contentment. If nothing disturbs this source, if it keeps its purity, if too much earth or sand does not fall into it . . . Otherwise, we feel its sweetness and refreshment and are watered by it only when it overflows.

To be tragic, misfortunes must be rare.

The truth! Only God sees it.

. . . Like those flashes of sharp light that suddenly enter a dark room.

——maxims, because what is isolated can be seen better.

In fact, goodness undoubtedly makes us better than morality.

To finish! What a word. We finish nothing when we stop, when we say we have come to the end.

What makes us look for a long time is that we do not look where we should or that we look where we should not. But how to look where we should when we do not even know what we are looking for? And this is what always happens when we compose and when we create. Fortunately, by straying in this fashion, we make more than one discovery, we have good encounters, and often are repaid for what we have looked for without finding by what we have found without looking for.

Reminiscence is an operation whereby the mind picks up the trail of its memories in order to find the memory it has lost.

Here I am outside civil things, in the pure region of Art.

(In a dream.) To unite matter to forms, which are the purest, the most beautiful, the truest things in nature. (Written at night, without being able to see.)

Dry, not like wood, but like bread. That is to say, dry, but nourishing, dry but not hard, not arid.

Necessity can make a doubtful action innocent, but it cannot make it commendable.

——and the pernicious habit of accepting pleasures without gratitude.

Poets—and the images of objects help them more than their presence.

To be the soul of a body, but not the head, that is a noble ambition.

Sloth waiting for inspiration.

The breath of the mind is attention.

The paper is patient, but the reader is not.

. . . have built their power with dead bodies.

Animals love the people who talk to them.

The republic of ants and the monarchy of bees.

If we exclude the idea of God, it is impossible to have an exact idea of virtue.

The great inconvenience of new books is that they prevent us from reading old books.

This philosophy perpetually concerned with what we must believe, and never with what we must do, nor what we must be.

Voltaire had the soul of a monkey and the mind of an angel.

Freedom. The freedom to do something well. There is no need of any other kind.
    Truths. The truths that teach us to act well and to live well. There is no need of any other kind.

Abuse of words, foundation of ideology.

The punishment of those who have loved women too much is to love them forever.

Because to think of God we do not need our brain.

Everything we can measure seems small.

The century felt it was making progress by falling into the precipice.

Mme de Sévigné said that "the pen always has a great part in what we write." And language in what we say.

——singularly able to enter the ideas of others without ever leaving his own.

Tenderness is the repose of passion.

[1809]

——because the sublime gives a useful pleasure.

Whoever consults the light within himself (it is in everyone) excels at judging the objects this light illumines.

The ellipsis, favorable to brevity, saves time and space.

Of those who lie to deceive, and of those who lie to persuade truth.

A work is perfectly finished only when nothing can be added to it and nothing taken away.

He must not only cultivate his friends, but cultivate his friendships within himself. They must be kept, cared for, watered.

In raising a child, we must think of his old age. (Or: In raising childhood, we must think of old age.)

There is a degree of bad health that makes us happy.

We always lose the friendship of those who lose our esteem.

——When we will have lost our mortality . . .

Because in fact reason leads man back to his instincts.

——and the pain of the soul: to expiate the pleasures of the body.

Of those who have a visible soul.

Everything that becomes a duty should become dear.

There is an infinity of things that one does well only through necessity.

The talkative person is someone who speaks more than he thinks. Someone who thinks a great deal and who talks a great deal is never considered a talkative person. The talkative man speaks from his mouth, the eloquent man speaks from his heart.

[1810]

All cries and all complaints exhale a vapor, and from this vapor a cloud is formed, and from these heaped-up clouds come thunder, storms, the inclemencies that destroy everything.

Let's go; and follow your mistake.

Anger, which purges resentment.

[1811]

The bad must be changed into the good, the incomplete must be finished, and what is twisted must be straightened.

Credulity forges more miracles than trickery could invent.

Nothing corrects a badly made mind. A sad and irritating truth that we learn late and after so many wasted efforts!

[1812]

To let the reader sometimes complete the symmetry between words and to do no more than suggest it.

In this painting of our life given to us by our memories, everything is moving and depends on our point of view.

Ash Wednesday.
     The face. After the face, action. Between the two, attitudes.
But before everything, the idea.

And the sun, and its rays. And if, instead of touching you with
his glance, someone touched you with his eyes; and if with his
fingertip instead of his cane; and if with his hand and not with
his glove.

(Ætatis, ann. 58)
     Never the mind without the soul.

For the soul the mind is a sort of organ, a sort of eye, of language,
of hearing, and even a brain, a sort of megaphone, of telescope,
of compass. And sometimes this organ acts all on its own.

Having found nothing worth more than emptiness, he leaves
space vacant.

The ideas of eternity and space have something divine about
them, but not those of pure duration and simple extension.

——This great player of human chess.

The world is a drop of air.

A falling stone is animated by a kind of passion. It shatters not because of its weight, but because of the attraction that animates it, and this is a quasi-spiritual thing.

When I had the strength, I did not have the patience. I have the patience today and I no longer have the power.

The child must live with the world before living with society; and he must love his parents before loving his teachers and comrades.

——and to destroy my memory by my presence.

. . . and, how in everything I say my affections always come before my thoughts, and how I am still dominated more by a love for justice than a love for truth,—which is very inconvenient when one considers the objectivity needed to explain oneself.
(*Nota.* Marvejols.)

Reason is against, but experience is absolutely for something that happens often, and then experience should decide and have the upper hand.

These beautiful words of Chateaubriand: "This moderation . . . without which everything is a lie."

Fortunately, when he lacks reasons he also lacks words.

Poetry made with little matter: with leaves, with grains of sand, with air, with nothings, etc.

Of those who have a muse and those who have only their soul.

Of the friendship we have for an old man. We love him in the way we love a fleeting thing. He is a ripened fruit that we are waiting to see fall. It is like knowing someone in very bad health. These words of Epictetus are easily applied to him: —I saw what is fragile break.

India. A subject capable of providing a fine story and one that carries its poetry within itself. It concerns an unknown country, unknown men, unknown customs. We want the truth about it: fiction would spoil everything.

[1813]

Date locum irae. Let anger pass, make a place for it; do not impede its progress; do not disturb its development, give it the time it needs to die out, open a wide path for it.

Gray hair, mixture of strength and old age.

There are words agreeable to the eye (in the same way there are words agreeable to the ear). By a fortunate combination of the letters that form them or by the harmony of these letters. For each letter has its shape.

Silence.—Joys of silence.—Thoughts must be born from the soul and words from silence.—An attentive silence.

What I call "phosphorescent." Colored sounds.

In political institutions, almost everything we call an abuse was once a remedy.

This world, for the other.

"Leave behind endless hope and vast thoughts," says the poet. I no longer have vast thoughts.

What is clear should not be drawn out too much. These useless explanations, these endless examinations are a kind of long whiteness and lead to boredom. It is the uniformity of a wall, of a long piece of laundry.

In order to know men, something must be chanced. Who risks nothing of himself knows nothing.

To thank heaven when it gives us beautiful dreams.

——to dream of freshness. Who dreams of freshness feels it.

There are, following Plato's idea, souls that not only do not have wings but do not even have feet (for progress or consistency) or hands (for work).

Egregie fallitur. He is wrong, but nobly, intelligently, with grace, with spirit, with wisdom and much beauty.

You have put up limits in vain; we see space out there and run towards it. We would like to break through your bars.—Your *nec plus ultra* was written by pygmies.

There is a residue of wisdom (as there is a residue of madness); and in human wisdom this residue purified by old age is perhaps the best thing we have.

To be pathetic when we cry, we must cry without wanting to and without knowing it.

. . . draw the attention and hold onto it; also: satisfy it.

Half myself mocks the other half.

A frightening thing, which is perhaps true: "old men want to survive."

The rightness of a certain tact. Everything depends on it.

You want to explain everything by the facts that are known to you. But the facts that are not known to you? What do they say?

Peoples that have overthrown geography (like winds, storms, and torrents).

I can do something well only slowly and with great effort.
    Our moments of light are all moments of happiness. When it is bright in our mind, the weather is good.

[1814]

Nothing is better than a justified enthusiasm.

What leads us astray in morality is an excessive love of
pleasure; and what stops us or holds us back in metaphysics
is a love of certainty.

Our thoughts are sometimes an image of the world, sometimes
a product of our mind, and sometimes the result or fabrication
of our excited will. When they are an image of the world, they
paint the truth. If they are the simple product of our mind, they
represent our mind and paint something else as well. But if they
are the result or fabrication of our will alone, they paint nothing
true, nothing that can give pleasure. They are bizarre traits,
writer's caprices, mere pen scratchings. . . .

More than once I have brought the cup of abundance to my lips;
but it is a water that has always escaped me. (Another version:
I have often brought to my lips the cup that holds abundance;
it is a water that has always escaped me.)

In painting, the pure idea. In sculpture, a real base clothed by
an idea. In painting, shadow and idea; in sculpture, idea with
a body, the idea incorporated and not simply represented.
In sculpture, the expressed idea is all on the surface; in painting,

it must be within. Beauty is hollowed out in painting; in sculpture it is in relief.

——like those birds that never perch on anything but the peaks of the highest trees, on the tips of shrubs.

The end of life is bitter.

Bourgeois old age as compared to the old age of the poor.

Almost all men prefer danger to fear. Some prefer death to danger and to pain. This is because fear, danger, and pain disturb reason. The horse throws himself into the precipice to escape the spur.

He did not know how to do anything with just a little; neither with few men nor with little money. But such was his power that he took money and men and no one dared refuse him.

There is in each man a divine part that is born with him, and a human and even animal part that grows with time. The first must be conserved and carefully cultivated within ourselves, the other thrives without help.

In literature, beauty must not be fabricated.

The gleam of the diamond in the pearls of the dew.

Let us look for our lights in our feelings. There is a warmth in them that contains many clarities.

To put the soul into physics and the body into metaphysics, if we want the first to be true and the second to be believable. For in the physical world everything happens from such subtle causes and in the metaphysical world everything that happens should be similar to what we see, etc. . . . .

Remember that God gave us the power to imagine what our nature has not given us the possibility of seeing.

Fire, ignition, and brightness; the body, its shadow and penumbra; sound, echo, and half-echo: everything has some shadow, some glow or reverberation. (Reflection.)

Neither in the arts, nor in logic, nor in life should an idea in any way be treated as a thing.

There is nothing perfectly true for man; I mean in human opinions. Just as there is nothing perfectly round.

If it concerns an individual, there is no cause for abstraction. What is collective necessitates it, because every multitude forms a whole only through fiction.

——for I have a very loving head and a stubborn heart. Everything I admire is dear to me; and nothing that is dear to me can ever become completely indifferent to me.

Our life is of woven wind.

To speak to God of everything; to dare to question him and to be attentive to what he says about everything. But sometimes we take our own voice for that of God.

Sonorous prose. Is this an advantage or a drawback?

Courage (in a soldier) is maintained by a certain anger; anger is a little blind and likes to strike out. And from this follow a thousand abuses, a thousand evils and misfortunes that are impossible to predict in an army during a war.

Retreat often into your sphere, rest yourself in your center, plunge yourself into your element: good advice, which must be remembered.

Of the sincerity of things. To see it. Truth consists of this.

[1815]

I confess that I am like an aeolian harp—which gives off some pretty sounds but can play no songs.

Too much harmony. Prose can have too much of it; also too much sweetness. And this is a very seductive fault, at first very agreeable, but unbearable and ridiculous over the long term.
    Varnish (in style) makes a glaze (for the reader).

Tormented by the cursed ambition always to put a whole book in a page, a whole page in a sentence, and this sentence in a word. I am speaking of myself.

As the hands would feel it or the eye would see it; that is the great question.

Yes, light. But what does it shine on? It is beautiful even when it shines on nothing. And when it shines on evil? Even then it is beautiful; even if it shines on what is hideous.

Of the freedom of thoughts (and the freedom of words) in the development of a text. And how (or through what art, what practice, what turns of phrase) to keep the freedom of thoughts and words, to keep their detached and mobile air in the most easily followed and best constructed texts. *Nothing nailed down*: let us make these words a guiding principle.

I do not like philosophy (and especially metaphysics) that is four-legged or two-legged;—I want it to be winged and singing.
　　Let metaphysics therefore have wings.

You go to truth by way of poetry and I come to poetry by way of truth.

——always occupied with the duties of others, never his own, alas!

What is pleasing always has something chanced about it.

To write his views or his observations, his ideas, but not his judgments. Our judgments limit our views of things. Some enclosures, but no walls. The man who always writes his judgments places before his eyes the *calpe* and the *abyla*. He goes no farther and creates a *nec plus ultra*. Thus, in the study of wisdom, many views and few judgments.

Of light. Dry light, wet light, warm light. (It is less clear, but it has much more effect.) Cold light. This is the light of artificial elegance, which comes from an ability without genius and a taste without enthusiasm.

Lafontaine: His taste is never without enthusiasm; nor that of Fontanes either, in those verses he has written in spite of himself.

Beyond domestic affections, all long-term feelings are impossible for the French.

When laws ruin customs . . .

Without fixed ideas, no fixed feelings.

When we find what we have been looking for, we don't have time to say it. We must die.

All foods are in fact good for someone who is hungry, but not for someone who has no appetite.

Leave dreams of the imagination time to evaporate.

To seek that style which makes one perceive or discover more meanings than it explains.

It is probable that the eye of the bird takes pleasure in colors (those of flowers), in greenery, and even in the sparkling of water.

One must die lovable (if one can).

Reason does not reason. It goes straight to the fact or the consequence.

That: we cannot escape certain errors except from above, that is to say, in raising our mind above human things.—Through the roof or through what is high; through the window or through the wall; through the door or through ordinary solutions.

When a truth is better conceived through abstraction, use the abstraction; if not, don't.

France destroyed by its philosophers.

It is not light that burns, that purifies, that consumes, that divides, and that recomposes: it is fire. And this fire we are talking about always follows light.

Of what must be said and what must not be said. The importance of knowing.

Old age and its mask.

Everything is new. And we are living among events so singular
that old people have no more knowledge of them, are no more
habituated to them, and have no more experience of them than
young people.

We are all novices, because everything is new.

When you no longer love what is beautiful, you can no longer write.

In such times, if you want neither to lie nor to wound, you
are reduced to being silent.

When everything becomes unbearable . . . That is the rule.
Then necessity makes the law, or changes it.

[1816]

Plato. The poetic spirit that gives life to the languors of his
dialectic. He is lost in the void; but we can see his wings beating,
we can hear their noise. His imitators lack these wings.

A symmetry that everywhere makes itself felt and does not
show itself.

These simple foods. For it is not enough to live (or to eat them) with pleasure, but with joy.

[1817]

Melancholy: when we have sorrows without a name.

It is better to be concerned with being than with nothingness. Dream therefore of what you still have rather than of what you have lost.

God! . . . Always! always! Never—never—

[1818]

. . . to procure for himself a moment of beauty.

". . .What is involuntary in human nature." This "involuntary" is very true, very beautiful, very well observed; and this observation is new.

The two suns we have in our head.

You want to talk to someone: first open your ears.

I am an aeolian harp. No wind has passed through me.

Madness is an illness of the brain, not of the mind.

Then, God withdrew his forces into himself, and we grew old.

Luminous words, like those drops of light we see in fireworks.

If you want to think well, to write well, to act well, first make a "place" for yourself, a "true place." Because we lack true places, we put our thoughts outside the true light and our conduct outside order.

These heads in which all lights have been extinguished, like these lanterns . . .

[1819]

Happy is the man who can do only one thing: in doing it, he fulfills his destiny.

Of the silence and darkness that surround the laws.

Don Quixote going to Tobosa and talking to Sancho as Socrates did to his disciples; and this is not ridiculous and does not even seem out of place.

Because they know all the words, they think they know all the truths.

There are things we can speak of only in writing, that we cannot know except when thinking of writing them down, and that we cannot, however, think of writing except when we know them in advance.

[1821]

And the most terrible, the most horrible of catastrophes imaginable, the conflagration of the universe, can it be anything more than the crackling, the burst, and the evaporation of a grain of powder on a candle?

God will draw in his breath and the whole world will disappear. No more theater, no more actors, no more spectators; smoke, and the smoke of a breath, the warmth of a breath.

[1823]

And perhaps there is no advice to give a writer more important than this: —Never write anything that does not give you great pleasure.

Spaces . . . I would almost say . . . imaginary; existence is so much in them, etc.

[1824]

Nota.— The true—the beautiful = the just—the holy—

***

Stéphane Mallarmé

A Tomb for Anatole

***

child sprung from
the two of us — showing
us our ideal, the way
— ours! father
and mother who
    sadly existing
survive him as
the two extremes —
badly coupled in him
and sundered
— from whence his death — o-
bliterating this little child "self"

     (3
better
as if he (when)
still were —
whatever they may have been,
of epithets
worthy — etc.
the hours when
you were and
were not

sick in
      springtime
dead in fall
     — it is the sun

        ————

     the wave
idea   the cough
2

son
     reabsorbed
not gone
    it is he
— or his brother
      myself
       I told this
         to him
two brothers
     —

forced back remaining
in the womb —
⟨only⟩ upon myself
      century
will not flow out
only
      to instruct me.

    did not know
mother, and son did
not know me! —
    — image of myself
    other than myself
      borne off
      in death!

        what has taken refuge
your future   in me
         becomes my
purity through life,
which I shall not
   touch —

there is   era of
       one
Existence in which we will
  find ourselves,
    if not a place —
— and if you
    doubt it
    the world will
    be the witness,
assuming that
  I live to be that old
    ——

pref.

father who
born in a bad
time had
prepared for son —
a sublime task

—

"the double one to
be filled — the child's
his own — the pain the desire
to sacrifice himself to one who is
no more will they triumph over
strength (the man he did not become)
and who will carry out the child's task

the supreme goal
would only have been
to leave life
pure
        you did this
in advance
    by suffering
      so much — sweet
      child so that
It will count against
your lost life — your family
has bought the rest by their
            suffering from having you
                  no longer

(I

to pray the dead
(not for them)

—

   knees, child
   knees — need
to have the child here
  — his absence — knees
fall — and

—

for one of the true dead
only a child!

(2

  hands join
towards the one who can
  not be touched —
  but who is —
  — that a space
  divides —

(1
Pref.

dear one

— great heart
⟨tr⟩ truly son of ⟨who⟩
                father whose
heart
beat for things
    too vast
    — and which came here
    to fail
        it was necessary —
inheriting this
marvelous fil-
ial intelligence, making

(2

it live again
— to construct
with his ⟨clear⟩
lucidity — this
work — too
    vast for me

and thus, (robbing
me of
life, sacri-
ficing it, if it

(3
is not for the wk
— to be him grown up,
⟨robbed⟩ of — and
to do this without
fear of <u>playing</u>
with his death —
since I
sacrificed my
life to it — since
I myself
took on this death
     (cloistering)

example
   we have known
through you this "better
part of ourselves"
which often
escapes us — and will be
within us — and our
acts, now
—

child, planting
   idealization

father and mother
 vowing
 to have no other
 child
   — grave dug by him
    life ends here

  vain
    cures
      abandoned
 if nature
 did not will it
—
   I will find them
   to work against
   death

balms, only,
consolations for us
  — doubt
then no! their reality

child our
immortality
  in fact made
of buried human
hopes — son —
entrusted to the woman
by the man de-
spairing after youth
to find the mystery
and taking a wife

    —

                              (1
sick
      since the day when death
moved in — marked by
sickness —
already is no longer himself, but
is the one through
death we would later
want to see again —
summing up death and
corruption — appearing
like that, with his sickness
      and his pallor

(2

⌈ sick — to be naked
⌊ like the child —

and appearing before us
— we take advantage of these
hours, when death
                     struck down
he lives
        again, and
   again is ours

title poetry of
        the sickness.

(1

with gift of word
I could have made you
            you,   the child of the wk.
   king   made of you
                     instead
— no, sad   of the son
                     in us
   — made you   — of
                     task
            no   —

                     no he
   remember the   proves
                     he was
   bad days —   that —
                     played
   mouth shut, etc. this role!
            natal
— etc.   word   —
                 forgotten
   it is I who
   have helped you since

(2

— have carried in
you the child —
    youth or curse
  of the story learned
    forgotten   from which
                         nothing

    I would not have
suffered — to be
in my turn
studying only that
— etc. (death

⟨3

then — you would not then have been
  other than myself
  — since I am
here — alone, sad —
— no, I
  remember a
  childhood —
    — yours
      two voices)

_____

but without you
I wouldn't have — known

⟨4

before doing the
  +   )
⟨thus it is⟩
  thus it is me,
cursed hands —
who has bequeathed you!
  — silence
  (he forgives)

(5

Oh! leave. . . us
on this word
  — which mingles
  the two of us
  together
  — unites us
  finally —
    for who said
it
      yours)

(1

cruel
etc.
  trappings
Oh! allow — no
you still want. . .

ancient egypt —
embalmings —
days, operations
crypts — all this
change

(2

once barbarous and
           external
   matter —
now
    moral

and within us

             want
   to thwart death
——

⟨Oh⟩ hear the cries
      of woman
Oh! I admit
you are strong, clever —
   etc.

brother sister
not ever the absent one
———
will not be less than
the one present —

to feel it burst
⟨the vo⟩ in the night
the immense void
produced by what
would be his <u>life</u>
— because he does not
<u>know</u> it —
that he is dead
lightning?
attack
pain

(1
moment when we must
break with the
living memory,
to bury it
— put it in the coffin,
hide it — with
the brutalities of
putting it into the coffin
raw contact, etc.

(2
so as not to see it anymore
        except idealized —
afterwards, no longer him
alive there — but
seed of his being
taken back into itself —
seed allowing
to think for him
— to see him ⟨and to⟩

(3

vision (ideality
of the state) and to
speak for him
—
for in us, pure
him, purification
— become our
honor, the source
of our finest
feelings — etc

(4

{ + true return
into the ideal}

—————————————

treacherous blow
of death — of
    without his
evil
      knowing anything
— in my turn
to play with it, even
though the child knows
nothing

time of the
   empty room
—

    until we
       open it
perhaps all
    follows from this
    (morally)
    ———

he knows nothing of it!
— and mother weeps —
     idea there
yes, let us take everything
on ourselves, then his
life — etc. —
for sinister
   not to know
      and to be no more.

    —

                 (1
you can, with your little
hands, drag me
into your grave — you
have the right —
— I
who follow you, I
let myself go —
— but if you
wish, the two
   of us, let us make. .

(2
an alliance
a hymen, superb
— and the life
remaining in me
I will use for — — — — —

and no mother
    then?

(1
    ceremony —
      casket —
      etc.
      we saw there (the father)
      the whole material side
who allows himself
to say if need be
  ah! yes! all
is there — ⟨and perhaps⟩
no fear for me
to think of something else
(the reformation

(2

of his spirit that is
eternal — can
wait
  ⌈ be but eternity
  ⌊ throughout my life
——

father —
to create his spirit
(he absent, alas!
as we would have
formed him present
——— better
              but

(3

sometimes when all
seems to go
too well — thus in
ideal —
  to cry out   —   ⟨it is not⟩
  in the mother's tone, who she
has become attentive —
It is not all that, no
I want him, him — and
     —

not myself —

(1

you look at me
I still cannot tell you
the truth
        I do not dare, too little one
What has happened to you
—

one day I will
tell you
        — for man
I do not want

(2

you not to know
your fate
—

and man
dead child

no — nothing
to do with the great
deaths — etc.
— as long as we
go on living, he
lives — in us
—

it will only be after our
death that he will be dead
— and the bells
of the Dead will toll for
                    him

                    (1
little
    virgin
    betrothed life
    that would have been
    a woman
—

let me tell you
the things you are
missing from
    — but

Oh! leave
us   cemetery
father
— and let us speak
of what
the two of us
    know
        mystery

        sail —
            navigates
            river,
    your life that
    goes by, that flows

        —

Oh! make us
                    suffer
    you who do not
    doubt it
much — all
that ⟨he⟩ equals
your life, painful in
                    broken
us
—

    while
    you glide, free

What! this day of
the dead — for him —
him —

The sacrifice
   of the child

   so that earth
   — mother — task
city men

end of I
— o terror
      he is dead!
      ____

   he is. . . dead
   (absolutely —
   i.e. struck
   the mother sees him in such

a way that,
   sick, he seems
to come back — in the future —
   or their race secured
            in the present

    mother I
one cannot
die with such
eyes, etc.

   ——

father lets escape
in his horror,
sobs
        "he is dead"
— and it is in the wake
of this cry, that
II the child

                     (2

    stands up on his bed
he looks, etc.

   ——

    in III perhaps
nothing — ⟨positive⟩
              on death
and
   simply
  stated — in
    the space of "he is
       dead of I II

    ——

The father looks —
and stops —
the child being
there, still, as if
to take hold of life again
— now interruption
in the father — and the
mother appearing hopes
cares —   the double side
                man woman
                — soon in
profound union
                the one, in the other, from which

                        (1

and you his sister,
you who one day
— (this gulf open
since his death and
that will follow us
until our own —
when we will
have descended there
your mother and I)
must one day

(2

unite all three
of us in your thought,
your memory —— —
—   just as in
      a single tomb
   you who, following
the order, will come
upon this tomb, not
made for you —

   Setting sun
and wind
   now vanished, and
wind of <u>nothing</u>
<u>that breathes</u>
(here, the modern
? nothingness)

tears, influx
                  the
of lucidity, dead one
is seen again
sheer through

——

                                        (1

death — whispers softly
   — I am no one —
     I do not even know who I am
    (for the dead do not
    know they are
    dead —, nor even that they
                 die
     — for children
    at least
        — or

            (2
heroes — sudden
deaths

for otherwise
my beauty is
made of last
moments —
lucidity, beauty
face — of
what would be

           (3
me, without myself
—

for as soon as
        (as one is
I am — ⟨I⟩
dead) I cease
to be —
—

thus made of
forebodings, of in-
tuitions, supreme

(4
shudders — I
am not —
        but at the ideal
   state
   ‾‾‾‾‾

and for the
others, tears
mourning, etc —

and it is my

(5
shadow not knowing
who I am, who
dresses in mourning
        ‾‾‾
the others —
   ‾‾‾‾‾
⟨tears, no more⟩
        ——⟨nor⟩
⟨others⟩ — — —
        ⟨from which came⟩

(1

Notes
————

whatever poem
based on facts
always — should
take only
general facts —
it happens here
that taken to-
gether harmonize

(2

often with the
last ⟨destiny⟩ moments of the
delightful child —

thus father —
      seeing that he
      must be dead

—

      mother, supreme
      illusion, etc.

death — purification
image in ourselves
purified by   ⌈and before
                |image
tears   ——   ⌊also —
simply remains
not to touch —
but to speak —

                    (1
    II   general effect
⟨he must⟩
is he dead? (i.
e. struck to death
⟨no⟩
    and is he coming back already
(in the space of the
must die)
    from the terrible future
that awaits him?

⟨II⟩   (2

or is he
still sick?

—

  sickness one
  clings
  to, want-
  ing it
  to last, to have him
  longer

—

   now <u>death</u>

(3

"why stop me
from making you
worried — sad —
distorted — while
I mold him
for the beautiful and sacred
day when he will not
suffer anymore —   [on the

(4

death bed —
⟨he who⟩ but
mute, etc. — instead
of formerly I —
perhaps what
will go in I —
  "Oh! if he ever
died — — — — —
     mother

(5

does not end —
— the father and mother
are needed?
  who both find
themselves before
sepulchre — without him
ah! well —?

(1
                seated, dreamer
⟨not to⟩   talking
                        with him
    not to feel you on
my knees, that
means they slip away
and that I am
kneeling
    — no longer before
    the familiar child
    etc. — then, with
            ⟨but the⟩

(2
    his jacket — (sailor?)
but before
    the young god,
hero, made holy through
death —

family perfect
balance
   father son
   mother daughter

broken —
three, a void
among us,
        searching. . .

     much better
that he not know it
   —
   we take on all
   tears
       — weep, mother
   etc.
 — transition from one
  state to the other
   thus not dead
death — ridiculous enemy
  — who cannot inflict on the child
   the notion that you exist!

death is   prayer
             of mother
nothing   — playing
                  death
      ⟨remedies⟩ she
    "so that the child
      does not
             know

 —

  and father benefits.

no more life for

 —

me
      and I feel
I am lying in the grave
beside you.

or: ordinary
Poem
It is true
you have struck me
and you have carefully chosen
your wound —
— etc.
— but

————

and vengeance
struggle between spirit and
death

(1

death
there are only conso-
lations, thoughts — balm

but what is done
is done — we cannot
hark back to the absolute
stuff of death —

— and nevertheless
to show that if,
once life has been

(2

abstracted, the happiness of being
together, etc — this
consolation in its turn,
has its foundation — its base —
absolute — in what
(if we ⟨ma⟩ want
for example that a
dead being lives in
us, thought —
it is his being, his

(3

thought in fact —
what is best in him
that happens, through our
love and the care
we take
of his being —
    [being, not being
       more than moral and
        as for thought]

in this there is
a magnificent beyond

(4

that rediscovers its
truth — so much more
pure and beautiful than
the absolute break
of death — little by little
become as illusory
as absolute (from which one is
allowed to seem
to <u>forget</u> the pains
etc —)

(5

— just as this illu-
sion of survival in
us, becomes the absolute
illusion — (there is ⟨being⟩
unreality in the two
cases) was terrible
            and true,

            ———

the father alone
    the mother alone
—

    each hiding from
    the other
    and found again
          —

     ————

together

o earth — you do not
   grow anything
— pointless
— I who
   honor you —

bouquets
   vain beauty

friends
    mysterious finger
  shown

    appeared
— chasing away
      the false

    —

⟨little⟩
        of vain
         source
  stays there —   dead?
  be!
  and that life will pass
—— river
    beside him
  protected by harsh nature

——

the little one fallen
    into the valley

  purity
double
  — identity

  —

  the eyes
two equal
points of view

  his eyes look
at me, double
  and sufficient
  — already claimed by
absence and the
  gulf

—

to bring everything together here?

(1

man and
absence —
  the twin
spirit he unites
with when he
dreams, longs

— absence, alone
after death, once

(2

  the pious
  burial of the
body, makes myste-
  riously — this
admitted fiction —

The sacrifice —
    on the tomb
why + , love
    mother
    it is necessary
      — so that he might be
again! (transfusion)
    mother alone wants
      to have him, she is earth
      —

    Since it is <u>necessary</u>
    What are you saying there —
do not interrupt me —

I

mother's fears
   — he stopped
    playing
    today

father listens — sees
  the mother's eyes
— allows to be cared for II
and dreams
    —

II

mother's tears
    room
  little by little calming down
    in the double
    point of view
     child, destiny
    —

    tomb, memory
old man —
     — (who speaks)

I   mother's cry
flowers
  gathered for
      tomb, left there

III
tomb
  father —

slow to sacrifice
    earth alters him
during this time

    other mother
      (mother says nothing?)

    mute and eternal
          pain.

(1

  if he heard us
how vexed he would be
  —

  to suppress him
like this
   sacrilege without
            tomb
  that he know it!
           shadow
—

no, divinely
     for not dead
  and in us
        — the

(2

transfusion —
  change in the manner
  of being, that's all

what!
    to rejoice in
presence
    and to forget him
    when absent
— simply! ingratitude!
    no — "hold" on
the life" of the being
who was — absolute
    —

Bitterness and
need for revenge
when he
seems to protest

        ———

desire to do
nothing anymore — ⟨nothing⟩
to miss the sublime
goal, etc. —

what! enormous
  death — terrible
  death
—

    to strike down
      so small a creature
—

I say to death   coward

  alas! it is within us
not without

he has dug our
  grave
     in dying

  has granted it

III
Friend

—

the friend — — — —
burial at the moment of seeing
the child ,
you alone do not know it —
— you look at me
how are still
stunned
you — close these sweet eyes
— not know — I
take care of it — continue
and you will live —

(1

to see him dead
— mother's fears
on the funeral bed
from the moment the playing
stopped in I
— end of I
break
voice that cries until
then — for the dead child

(2

and to join — eyes
closed — father —
   (mother closed them —
"not to know where he
is", to bury him in
  the shadow
    — struggle, struggle

      —

Oh! how the eyes of the dead
etc.
    have more strength
than those, the most beautiful eyes
of the living
  —

    that they would lure you in

    — —

 Breaking off from I
 to III
child dies then

 III (to speak
 often to him
I take you my child,

—

room ardent thought
— burial
 in — — —
II tears of the two
 hidden
I and one from the other

 III
tomb — ⟨goes⟩ fatality
— father — "he had
 to die —"
 mother does not want
 anyone to talk like this
 about her offspring —
— and father returns
to fulfilled des-
tiny in the form
 of the child

III

earth speaks —
      mother confused with
earth
through ditch dug
      by child — where
she will be — — —
      later —

      child
sister remains, who
will lead to a future
brother
    — she exempt from
this grave for
father mother and son
— by her marriage.

suffering — not vain
tears — falling
in ignorance — but
emotion, ⟨you n⟩ nourish-
ing your shadow
that comes to life in us

—

setting it up

—

life-giving tribute
   for him —

don't cry so loudly
   he will hear —

——

daughter struck dumb

What! was he born then for
                    mother
not being   too beautiful
                            too
    and the father's terror
    cursing his blood

— the mother — yes, made
for being, his eyes — to what
good such worry —
        he will live! (last cry)
                        treatments, etc.

        at least death
takes the meaning that he

(2
or mother
knows it
(sometimes, he turns away
from me,

and such terrible sacrifice

— father will unite
everything later in
prolonging
his being,
reabsorbing
etc.

Silent father
    opening of thought
—

    oh! the horrible secret
I carry inside me
        (what to do about it
—

    will become
       the shadow of his
        tomb
not known —

   —

    that he must
     die

after-effect
  ⟨immortality⟩
    eternity
  ⟨pre⟩ thanks to
    our love
— he prolongs us
  beyond
      —

      (in exchange
      we give him back
        life

  in filling ourselves
    with thought

tenderly: we must not
　　　　　　　cry anymore
let us cry no more
look at you
　　　　man
　　— I can tell you
　　　　what you do not know
that you were betrayed —
　　　　falsehood, etc —

———————————————————

old +
　god of his race
　　　　　　　— as poet
　— the one who　　　not
　　　　　　　— as man
　stirs
　　　each of our gestures
　　　　　　　　　　etc.
　　　　　— gold!

              after, no you will not
                        take him
Yes —   (1
        I recognize
your power o death

stealthily
    — you took him —
he is now only spirit
in us — etc.
powerless against human kind
    but   human death
    as long as humanity
    century stone tomb

                    (stop
earth — open ditch
never to be filled
    — except by sky
    — indifferent earth
        grave
            not flowers
    bouquets, our
    festivals and our life

(1

little child
   that death can take
the ignorant
    — but young
afflicted man — already
in him — I do not dare
endure this look
filled with the future
     — oh! good, <u>evil</u>

race in
   me —
   that this look
follows beyond into
(absolute) future
our reunion

———

must it —
   by what ritual?
   to inhume in the name
of race, ancestors, with

(3
immortality
— or mine
new —

(1
cemetery
the need to go there
to renew
laceration
pain — through
the dear being
idea of ⟨death⟩ there
———

when the too powerful
illusion of having him
always with us

no, you are not one of the dead
— you will not be among
the dead, always in us

(2

becomes a
delight (bitter enough
point) for us —
and unjust for the one
who remains below, and is
in reality deprived
of all that
we connect him with.

———

mother identity
   of dead life
      father picks up
 rhythm started here
of mother's
 rocking
   suspense — life
    death —
poetry — thought

(1

no death — you will not
deceive him —
— I take advantage of the fact
that you deceive him
— for his happy
   ignorance
  — but on the other hand
I take it back from you
    for the ideal tomb

(2

I want to suffer everything
⟨— ain⟩ for you
   who do not know —
   nothing will be
taken away (but
you) from the hideous mourning

— — —

and it's me, the man
you would have been

——

— for I will, from

(3

this mo-
ment on ⟨the⟩ be to you
— —

father and mother
   together
      their love

      idea of the child

to mother
   yes, weep
      — I however think

(1

Tomb

—

I. what! . . . here the sob
  the indignant protest
          hurled out to infinity
II. to take on oneself
  all his suffering
  a method —
and III. then, one can, eyes
  lifted to the sky —

———————————

draw the final line, calm
of the heavy tomb —

(2

—

gravely   —
such a painful thing
before ————
but not without
(sacrifice of
delights?) again
throwing on this
⟨rigid⟩ sinister line
of erasure   .
the last lamented flowers
once meant for him

(1

Indeed Sir
  indeed you are
        dead
  At least that
  is what your announcement
  letter

   ———

   and laughter from within
  myself — hideous!
in writing this as
your faithful servant —
      you who will see
clearly, o my — dearly

(2

beloved — that
if I could not
embrace you
squeeze you in
my arms
— it is because you were
inside me

Dear companion of the
hours I used to call
bad, and no
less later of those
I later call

(1

myself —
    perhaps —
the ambiguity
    this can be!

(2
pain ⟨and⟩ and sweet
   delights
      of the suffering
     ghost

mother
  he will not live!
———
two
—
father, in front of
      tomb
(mother to side?
   then comes back?

3rd part

  — the sacrificing father
      prepares himself —
but idea remains and
      of him
to construct everything on it —

      an offering to the absolute

2nd part

bitter
  — ah! so much the better that
not man
      but his eyes. . .
      but his mouth
— that spoke in this way? perhaps
his lover.
—

o lover, daughter I would have
loved
—

return to mother?

2nd part

seen, come back dead, through
illness — eyes, agree
to pour out light.
     — pretend
to play along, indifferently
——

   he knows without knowing
   and we weep for him without
letting him know

  enough tears — it is
to introduce death —

1st part

——

one feels — fatal blow
illuminating the soul —
that death —
   and (thunder) everything that
tumbles down
   ——

   dreams of leaving him a name, etc.

     already so changed that
it is no longer him —
     and the <u>idea</u> (of him) <u>yes</u>!
in this way little by little
comes through.

    ——

later, from the moment
that death hovers ——

    sick
       considered
         as dead
we already love the objects
"that remind us of him!"
          to set them in order

——————

and sometimes hope
        kills this fiction
           of death
  "no — he will live! —

life sheltered in us
where our life is dread
  horror of hole
    clings

———

to sacrifice it —

—

or poems, for
later, after
us, death —
  being

      that future eyes
  filled with earth
    never
cloud over
  with time

  —

I cannot believe
all that has
happened —
——— To
   begin again
in spirit beyond —
    the burial

           etc —

           dead!
Oh! you believe that
you will take him from me
thus — from this
mother
    — from me
       father

———

I admit that you can
        do much

(1
what do you want, sweet
adored vision —
who often come
towards me and lean
over — as if
to listen to secret {of
my tears} —
to know that you are
dead
— what you do not know?
— no I will not

(2
tell it
to you — for then you
would disappear —
and I would be alone
weeping, for you, me,
mingled, you weeping for
child
in me
the future
man you will not
be, and who remains
without life or joy.

———

vision
endlessly purified
by my tears

———

                    end of I

    pro-   ⎡He, dead —
    cess   ⎢   ⟨seen⟩ so beautiful
              ⎣child
      — and that the savage
                    dread
      of death fall on
      him {disturbed by
      mother's cry} with
      the man he should have
      become {seen in this
                    supreme instant}

to render death bed

oh — provided
that he knows nothing
of it — does
not doubt

—

{during sickness
— but from which treason
unknown
death —

no, I can
not throw earth
of oblivion

— — —

{earth mother
take him back
in your shadow

—

and his spirit
in me as well}

mother has bled and wept
father sacrifices — and deifies

II

not me —
  in myself —
  ———

and absence —
———

  oppos. IV or +
  the always
    self, nothing
              that we
but self!   love —
torturing the delicate
      soul

              (1
imply
perhaps the
ceremony
— funeral
etc — in brief what
people saw —
(burial
  mass?

  to carry this

(2

to intimacy
— the room —
empty — absence —
open — the
moment when his
absence ends,
so that he may be
in us —
—

that will be this
3rd part —

(3

after he has been
carried away, ⟨end of I⟩
out of the room —

— to see then
how II — "the
⟨which will be the⟩
⟨of⟩ sickness and
the little phantom" —
would be framed —
— III ghost

(4

above, towards
the end of II —
dead —

in this way furniture
immortality
—

and heart of nature
I — he will not play
anymore — merging
with countryside
    where he rests?
—

to specify?

        Ah! adorable heart
    o my image
    placed among the too vast
    destinies —
        only a child
        like you —
                I dream
                        still
            all alone — —
        in the future —

          ⟨1

Oh! you understand
that if I consent
to live — to seem
to forget you —
it is to ⟨so that⟩
feed my pain
— and so that this apparent
forgetfulness
    can spring forth more
horribly in tears, at

        ⟨2

some random
  moment, in
  the middle of this
  life, when you
  appear to me.

(1
time — that body
takes to decompose
in earth — (min-
gling little by little
with neutral earth
at the vast horizons)

it is then that he
lets go of the pure
spirit that we

(2
were — and which was
tied to him, orga-
nized — which
can, pure take
refuge in us,
to reign
⟨sit on throne⟩ in us,
survivors
— {or in

(3
absolute purity,
on which
time pivots and
is formed again —
　{once ⟨in⟩ God}
　was the most divine

─────

I who know it
for him　　carry a
　　　　　terrible
　　　　　secret!
　father —
　he, too much
child for
such things

─────

　I know it, it is in
this that his being is
perpetuated —

I feel it in me
who <u>wants</u> — if not
the lost life,
at least the equi-
valent —

death
— or one is stripped
of a body
  — in those who remain

                   (I
and then III
   to speak to him in this way
     is it not that
Friend, ⟨say that⟩
you triumph
⟨is it⟩ is it not
detached from ⟨your⟩ all
⟨my⟩ weight of
life
— from the old
pain of living
     (oh! I

(2

    feel you
so strongly — and that you
are always
well with
us, father, mother,
⟨meadows⟩ — but
free, eternal
child, and everywhere
at once —
    ———

  and the underside
     — I can

(3

say that because
I keep all my
pain for us —
— the pain of
not being — that
you do not know
   — and that I
impose on myself
   (cloistered, further-
more, outside of

(4
life where you
lead me
    (having opened
for us a
world of death)
        ——

                    (1
moral
burial
——   father mother
Oh
    do not hide
him yet,
    etc. ——

friend earth awaits
—— the pious act, of
hiding him
            —— lets

(2

the other mother —
common
to all men —
  {in which goes
the bed — where he is
now}
take him
— lets the
men who have appeared
— oh! the

(3

men — these
  men {under-
takers — or
friends?}
    carry him away
followed by tears
  — etc —
towards earth
mother of all

(4
mother of all — his
now
        and
(since she already
  partakes of <u>you</u>, your
  grave dug by
  him?)
        he
now become a face
    little man
    somber like a man
    —————————

        accomplices
            of death
it is
            during
            sickness
            — I
            thinking
              mother — ?
            and knowing

      to close his eyes
— I do not want
to close his eyes —
        — that will look
    at me always

———

  or death aside
    closed eyes, etc.
  we see him again in sickness
struggling against this horrible
state —

      little body
   put to the side
  by death
  a hand

that a moment
  before was him

— and cry, almost without
paying attention to this
body put aside —
     O my son
  as toward a heaven
  spiritual instinct

suspense
    — break —
     part
—

Oh! this sacrifice —
for that to deny
his life
    — to bury him
—

  let us talk about him
again, let us extinguish
  — in reality, silence

(1
    break   in two

I write — he
      (underground)
          decomposition
mother sees —
        what she should
                not know
——

  then sickness he comes back
up until ⟨com⟩, all
purified! (by disease) and
asleep — so beautiful dead
— tomb only a fiction
(we make him disappear —
so he will remain in

                              (2
us
      his look
                        (conscience)
— for a long time
watched during
  sickness
  ———

  or then
    triumph
  after —
                        3rd part
break between I and II
  and between ⟨II and IV⟩
              II and III
    everything connects again
                        —

not to know his
happiness
    when he is
there — . . . found that
so natural

  —————

     link
        to unconsciousness
       of death —

true mourning in
  the apartment
— not cemetery —

    furniture

to find <u>absence</u>
 <u>alone</u> —
    — in presence
of little clothes
 — etc —
            mother.

/

            little sailor —
sailor suit
           what!
— for enormous
               crossing
a wave will carry you
                ascetic
      sea,
           ⟨+ +⟩

(1

fiction
  of absence
      maintained by mother
—   apartment
⟨no⟩   "I do not know
        what they have
        done — ⟨I have not⟩ in
        the trouble and
        tears of that time
      —   I only

—————

but she followed to the cemetery.

(2

know that he is no longer
here

  and if, he is there — absent —
from which mother herself
has become phantom —
spiritualized by
habit of living
with a vision

(3

while he
father — who
built the
tomb —
  walled up . . . . .
           knows
— and won't his spirit
go looking for
the traces of
          and trans-
  destruction —   mute into
          pure
          spirit?

(4
with the result that
  purity emerges from
  corruption!

no — I will not
allow
  nothingness
   ——

   father —— — I
feel nothingness
  invade me

   and if at least
    — spirit —
   I have not given
   adequate blood —
      —
    that my thought
    make for him a
    purer more
      beautiful life.
    ——

— and like his fear of me — who
thinks — beside him —

What, the thing I am saying
is true — it is not
only
music ———
etc.

bouquets

we feel obliged
to throw into this earth
that opens in front
of the child — the most
beautiful bouquets —
the ⟨flowers⟩ most beautiful
products, of this
earth — sacrificed
— to veil

(2

(or have him pay
what he owes —

———

(1

II

struggle
   of the two
   father and son
  the one
to preserve son in
thought — ideal —
the other to
live, rising up
again etc —
  — interruptions
     deficiency)

—

(2

thus
   and mother cares
for him well —
   cares of mother
interrupting thought
     — and child
   between father who thinks
him dead, and mother
life —
——— "cares for him well
   etc.
     — from which

(3

It is only in III
that <u>burst</u> of this
(shattering) caused
by cry of I —
⟨and⟩ little by little
fits together —
all finished

child
          (m
destiny
earth calls it
consoling
   —

The grave father
  it is
    up to me
having given being
not to let him
be lost
    — trouble
and mother — I do not want
  him to stop
    (idea there!)

appeared!
   — shadow   (1
     my mother
     mother and son
        up to +

from the wretched day
and which I did
not doubt

                (2
if it is not
       punishment
   the children of other
            classes

———————

so that
   furious
   against +
     vile society
     that had to
          crush him
          perhaps

thus cured of an
    illness
    it catches up with me
    in this
      p.haps

* *

André du Bouchet

The Unihabited • Selected Poems

* *

v

FROM THE EDGE OF THE SCYTHE

I

The dryness that discovers the day.

To and fro, as the storm goes to and fro.

On a path that stays dry in spite of the rain.

The immense earth spills, and nothing is lost.

For a tear in the sky, the strength of the soil.

I quicken the bond of roads.

II

The mountain,
                    the earth drunk by the day, without
        the wall moving.

            The mountain
            like a fault in the breath

            the body of the glacier.

The clouds flying low, level with the road,
        lighting the paper.

I do not speak before this sky,
                            the tear,
                                    like
        a house given back to breath.

I saw the day shaken, without the wall moving.

III

The day scorches the ankles.

Keeping watch, shutters closed, in the whiteness of the room.

The whiteness of things comes out late.

                                        I go straight into the eddying day.

LAPSE

The shadow,

      shorter, the warmth, outside, replacing fire for us.

Nothing severs us from the warmth. On the hearth-ground,

through which I move,

      broken,

    toward these cold walls.

METEOR

The absence which takes the place of breath in me begins again like snow to fall upon the papers. The night appears. I write as far away from myself as possible.

ACCIDENTS

I wandered about this glow.
　　　　　　　I was torn again, from the other
side of this wall, like the air you see,
　　　　　　　　　　in this cold glow. From
the other side of the wall, I see the same blinding air.

　　　　　　　In the unbreached distance,
like the stretch of broken earth, beyond, I tread, nothing feels
the heat.

We will be washed of our face, like the air that crowns the wall.

THE WHITE MOTOR

I

I quickly removed
this sort of arbitrary bandage

I found myself
free
and without hope

like knotted sticks
or stone

I radiate

with the heat of stone

which resembles the cold
against the body of the field

but I know the heat and cold

the frame of the fire

the fire

in which I see
the head

the white limbs.

II

At several points the fire pierces the sky, the deaf side, which I have never seen.

The sky that heaves a bit above the earth. The black brow. I don't know if I am here or there,
                                    in the air or in a rut. They are scraps of air, which I crush like clumps of earth.

My life stops with the wall, or begins to walk where the wall stops, in the shattered sky. I do not stop.

III

My telling will be the black branch that forms an elbow in the sky.

IV

Here, its white mouth opens. There, it defends itself along the whole line, with these entrenched trees, these black beings. There again, it takes the hot, heavy form of fatigue, like limbs of earth, scorched by a plow.

I stop at the edge of my breath, as if beside a door, to listen to its cry.

Here, outside, a hand is upon us, a cold, heavy sea, as if, as the stones walk, we were walking with stones.

V

I go out
inside the room

as if outside

among the still
furnishings

in the shuddering heat

alone

outside its fire

there is not yet
anything

the wind.

VI

I walk, joined with fire, in the uncertain paper, mingled with air, the unprimed earth. I lend my arm to the wind.

I go no farther than my paper. Far before me, it fills a ravine. A bit farther, in the field, we are almost level. Half knee-deep in stones.

Nearby they speak of wounds, of a tree. I see myself in what they speak. That I not be mad. That my eyes not become as weak as the earth.

VII

I am in the field
like a drop of water
on a red-hot iron

the field itself
eclipsed

the stones open

like a stack of plates
held
in the arms

when evening breathes

I stay
with these cold white plates

as if I held the earth
itself

in my arms.

VIII

Already the spiders are running over me, on the dismembered earth. I rise above the plowing, on the clipped and arid runnels,

     of a finished field, now blue, where I walk without ease.

IX

Nothing satisfies me. I satisfy nothing. The bellowing fire will be the fruit of that day, on the fusing road, reaching whiteness in the battered eyes of stones.

X

I brake to see the vacant field, the sky above the wall. Between air and stone, I enter an unwalled field. I feel the skin of the air, and yet we remain divided.

Beyond us, there is no fire.

XI

A large white page, palpitating in the ruined light, lasts until we get closer to one another.

XII

In releasing the warm door, the iron knob, I find myself before a noise that has no end, a tractor. I touch the base of a gnarled bed. I do not begin. I have always lived. I see the stones more clearly. The enclosing shadow, the earth's red shadow on my fingers, in its weakness, beneath its draping, which the heat has not hidden from us.

XIII

This fire, like a smoother wall, built on top of another, and struck, violently, up to its peak, where it blinds us, like a wall I do not allow to petrify.

The earth lifts its harsh head.

The fire, like an open hand, which I no longer wish to name. If reality has come between us, like a wedge, and divided us, it was because I was too close to this heat, to this fire.

XIV

So, you have seen these burstings of the wind, these great discs of broken bread, in this brown country, like a hammer out of its matrix that swims against the unrippled current, of which nothing can be seen, but the gnarled bed, the road.

These keening bursts, these great blades, left by the wind.

The raised stone, the grass on its knees. What I don't know of the back and the profile, since the moment of soundlessness: you, like the night.

You recede.

This unharnessed fire, this unconsumed fire, igniting us, like a tree, along the slope.

XV

What remains after the fire are disqualified stones, frigid stones, the change of ashes in the field.

The carriage of the foam still remains, rattling, as if it had rushed forth again, from the tree, anchored to the earth with broken nails, this head, that emerges and falls into place, and the silence that claims us, like a vast field.

ANDRÉ DU BOUCHET

WHAT THE LAMP BURNED

Like a wound
again and again

the light

in which we sink

I began
by being

this tousled fuse

the earth

where the sleeve of the wind
is passing.

I dissipate, without renouncing my fire,

on a straight
slope.

Of stone. Today my mouth is new. At the beginning of the descent. I begin again.

Like a ceiling that is watched in a mirror, I unite the reflections of the mountain.

The light in the black part of the room, in the dimmed corner, where the table heaves.

A path, like a torrent without breath. I lend my breath to the stones. I move on, with shadow on my shoulders.

We recognize ourselves by our fatigue, the wood of limbs, the pyre, suddenly abandoned by the flame, and cold, at the bottom of the day. We shudder in the cold. Then I turned my back on those who embrace.

Our scythe straddles the country. We go faster than the roads. Faster than a car. As fast as the cold.

Already the country pierces. I do not stop. Through our face I see the path we did not take.

When I see nothing, I see the air. I grasp the cold by its handles.

GIVING OVER

The wind,
      in the waterless lands of summer, leaves us
           on a blade,
                  what is left of the sky.

In several cleavages, the earth reveals itself. The earth endures,
equal to itself, in the breath that strips us.

                Here, in the blue and motionless world,
I have almost reached this wall. The bottom of the day is still
ahead of us. The bottom of ignited earth. The bottom and
the surface of the brow,
           levelled by the same breath,
this cold.

I gather myself anew at the foot of this facade like the blue air at
the foot of the plowing.

                Nothing quenches my step.

TILL THE SUN

> Where the sun
> — the cold, earthen disc, the black and trodden disc,
> where the sun disappeared — upwards, into the air
> we shall not inhabit.

Sinking, like the sun,
whether we have disappeared — the work of the sun — or
again moving on.

Up to us — rugged road up to the brow.

I ran with the sun that disappeared.

Light, I've held my ground.

Up to the air we do not

breathe   —   up to us.

Tomorrow   —   already,

like a knot in the day. The halted wind thunders.

As, under the figure

of the sparse

air, in soils overturned upon it, straw, it,

sought by the wind, still   —

Uprooting itself, as I move on   —   uprooted
from its distances, the new soil, shot through with light.

Up to this earth inhabited under the step,
that dries up — only under the step.

Like the look
of what I have not seen — ahead as well.

Under the step, only, opening up to the day.

The face of water from glaciers. The face of water standing in the day.

But the earth, as long as I run,
is stopped under the wind.

Through the stones of waterless paths.   Stones half-way —

                                        In the day and its dust,
with the same step   —   upon us, cold, and breath, as if
hovering.

Through what gives, in the distance, another step (a burden
masking the fire,
                the cool)

                                        The air   —
without reaching the soil, even   —   under the step, returns.

THE UNINHABITED

We shall stop,
because of the height, in the wind that does not dry up distances,
on the stone-work standing.

Our support is heaving. The sky is full,
and opening again.

ANDRÉ DU BOUCHET

MARKING POSTS

Each closed upon the other   —
as, around the buried step, the sun,
short-lived earth.

The sun, still,
the sun, around this step, reverberates.

The vestige of the sun's step. Between us. Between sun and us.

Like the earth, then, on which will have passed   —   farther, I see it   —   the sun.

Straw in the thickness, on the whetstone
of a breath
that cuts, the slice!

Up to this distance it carries, it,
in the day. As I reach you.
But the vestige is still ahead of us.

Interrupted, as I meet you, where the day will have fused.

PLAIN

Grown until white

the age
the piece of earth
where I slip

as if radiating from cold

in the jolting day.

When I say coal
I want to say
winter

what it would have wanted to say
through this squall

the cough

contusions

everything set like a wound

the motionless plate

objects born from the hands
open
at the bottom of air

burning.

Chipped
by a tip-cart

the blue air

everywhere my brow
finds

the earth

or the brow of the earth.

In a cold
room
gilded from afar

the light is a fold

I see it
without sinking

almost under the wheels

like the mulberry
the road whitens.

POSTPONEMENT

Alone I inhabit this white
place

where nothing thwarts the wind

if we are what cried
and the cry

that opens this sky
of ice

this white ceiling

we have loved under this ceiling.

I almost see,
in the whiteness of the storm, what will come to pass without me.

I do not diminish. I breathe at the foot of arid light.

If there were not the force
of dust
that severs arms and legs

but only the white
that spills

I would hold the sky

deep rut
with which we turn

and which knocks against the air.

                        In this light that sun
abandons, all heat resolved in fire, I ran, nailed to the light
of roads, till wind buckles under.

Where I rend the air,
                        you have come through with me. I find you
in the heat. In the air, even farther, which uproots itself,
with a single jolt, away from the heat.

                        The dust lights up. The mountain,
frail lamp, appears.

THE LIGHT OF THE BLADE

This glacier that creaks

to utter
the cool of earth

without breathing.

Like paper flat against this earth,
or a bit above the earth,
like a blade I stop breathing. At night
I return to myself, for a moment, to utter it.

In place of the tree.
In the light of the stones.

I saw, all along the day,
the dark blue rafter that bars the day rise up to reach us
in the motionless light.

I walk in the gleams of dust
that mirror us.

In the short blue
breath
of the clattering air

far from breath

the air trembles and clatters.

THIS SURFACE

Of the earth,
I know nothing but the surface.

I have embraced it.

I have made my brow
out of this destruction

the cold
the summer revolving on it

from the day

this frayed wall
like a tongue that rasps

before it falls.

The lamp
is a cold fire,
then the cold comes out in the darkness.

While the gusts
of cold enter the room, I am still prey to this step, everywhere
I find the earth that comes before me and after me.

Warmer than I, the straw that envelops
our step emerging from earth — our step like this dawning
in the body

of earth.

PLOW-RIDGE

Flowers in the cold and rasping air
overturned upon us (I saw their step above)

As on roads the knee
bends,
the air　—　slower, farther,　—　sun after the day,
that breaks the breath.

The brow of the mountains comes in again. The cool
of the road revives.

Breath
on what the interrupted day

as glacier in the day

revives.

As
under the motionless foot
the soil without tie

the air.

Above the buried brow, brief surge, the trodden earth again closed.
The thinness of the other face   —   so thin that air can breathe   —
between sun and us.

                          Has slid. Between us has slid. The cold, then,
has slid.

                                 As, under the step,
    —   so much that air can breathe, between sun and us, the thin
earth.

Outside
                    where, upon what breathes,
the door, after the wind, will have shut, the air — where one
of us has disappeared. Air after the wind.

On the other side of this face,
as it will light up   —   on the other side of the dust,
the buried

sun.

Whoever speaks on interrupted air, the wind clasps him. The distant wind clasps him.

                                     Earth with breath
—   between sun and us   —   merged. But the sun that bears
away is half in the thickness.

                                     Where,
thrown — one of us, and the other   —   you draw up
this heat that knocks. As, around the soil of the shut earth, ahead
of us,
       our breath. Everything is yours. Is coming for you.

                                    The day

as, after oneself, the day.
               The wormwood. The comfrey
                              in its dust.

＊

Philippe Petit

On the High Wire

＊

DEFINITIONS

Whoever walks, dances, or performs
on a rope raised several yards from the ground
is not a high-wire walker.
His wire can be tight or slack; it can bounce
or be completely loose. He works with or without a balancing
pole.
He is called the ropedancer.

Whoever uses a thin wire of brass or steel
in the same way
becomes a low-wire artist.

There remains the one whose performance is a game of chance.
The one who is proud of his fear.
He dares to stretch his cable over precipices,
he attacks bell towers,
he separates mountains and brings them together.
His steel cable, his rope, must be extremely tight.
He uses a balancing pole for great crossings.
He is the *Voleur* of the Middle Ages,
the *Ascensioniste* of Blondin's time,
the *Funambule*.

In English we call him the High-Wire Walker.

WARNING

No, the high wire is not what you think it is.
It is not a realm of lightness, space, and smiles.
It is a job.
Grim, tough, deceptive.

And whoever does not want to struggle
against failure, against danger,
whoever is not prepared to give everything
to feel that he is alive,
does not need to be a high-wire walker.
Nor could he ever become one.

As for this book—
the study of the high wire is not rigorous,
it is useless.

SETTING UP THE WIRE

There are ropes made of natural fibers, artificial fibers, and metal fibers. When they are stretched, twisted, rolled, compressed, or submitted to rapidly changing temperatures, these fibers create a wire.

The wires are put together to form a strand. Several strands braided, twisted, or sheathed together become a rope. A rope often has in its center a strand of some other material. This is usually called the core, the "soul".

Wires, strands, and soul are assembled according to methods whose laws are as rigorous as they are varied.

The number of ropes, therefore, is infinite.

Whoever intends to master the art of walking on them must take on the task of seeking them out. Of comparing them. Of keeping those whose properties correspond to his aspirations. Of learning how to knot them. Of knowing how to tighten them.

Acquiring this knowledge is the work of a lifetime.

For now, take a metal rope of clear steel, composed of six, seven, or eight strands, with a diameter of between twelve and twenty-six millimeters.

With a soul of hemp.

Today, one no longer finds high-wire walkers who use thick ropes of Italian hemp. For reasons of convenience, the steel cable has replaced the rope.

This cable must be free of all traces of grease.

Each steel cable is lubricated when it is manufactured. The first operation, therefore, is to remove this grease. The best method is to stretch out the cable in the corner of a garden and to leave it there for several years. At the end of that time, you will hunt through the tall grass to retake possession of the "old" cable. To make it new again, wash it in gasoline and rub it with emery until it is clean and gray. It is a good idea to leave a considerable length of cable exposed in this fashion, perhaps five hundred meters. Walk-lengths can then be cut off when needed.

If you are not in a position to age a new cable in this manner, an alternative is to repeat the cleaning process as many times as necessary—to wipe each strand, one after the other, and to go through the operation again and again until the wire is absolutely dry. This method is not entirely satisfactory, however, since the grease that lurks in the soul can sometimes spill forth abundantly when a tightly stretched cable has been exposed to the sun for a prolonged period.

A rusted cable can be made excellent once it has been brushed and wiped.

A cable must be in good condition. Without kinks or meat hooks. Kinks are the traces left by an old loop or hook: the cable has been twisted, and when it is stretched out, a barely perceptible bump remains that even the greatest tension cannot eliminate. Meat hooks are the wires of a broken strand; they bristle up like splinters. To make sure that the cable is not concealing any meat hooks, run a cloth along the entire length of the wire in both directions.

When setting up for the first time, use a simple wire ten meters long, stretched out two and a half meters off the ground between two small poles—two X's of wood or metal—or, even more simply, between two trees. Preferably, trees with character. Attach one end with wire clamps; on the other end attach a tightening device (a large turnbuckle or a level hoist) to a sling. At the tip of the cable make a spliced eye with a thimble inside it. Draw the eye toward the hoist hook with the help of a pulley block. Fasten to the hoist and tighten. Be careful to wrap the tree trunks with large jute cloths so they are not hurt by the wire.

THE FIRST STEPS

The first steps, of course, can be made on a small wire stretched out just two inches from the ground. But then, you could just as easily close this book and become a weekend wire walker.

Don't look for a ladder; leap up onto the wire. Slippers and balancing pole are for later.

Right away, balance yourself on one foot, facing the tree. Quick. Try to hold on as long as possible before grabbing the tree again.

Do not jump. Do not walk. The leg is fixed. The foot is poised along the wire.

Your arms will wave about wildly. Pay no attention to them. Look for balance. Enough! Change feet. Just a little try. Change again. In this way you will find your better foot, the one that will later become your "balancing foot." Then you will stop these stupid gymnastics, turn around, and lean your back against the tree.

High-wire walking is not a solution to the problem of balance.

Look intensely at what stretches out before you.

You are facing the cable.

That's it.

Everything changes now that the wire is there.

Fix your eyes on the target—the end—and try a crossing.

Don't look for the bark behind you, but jump down the moment you lose your balance. In this way, the crossing will be a series of balancings: on one foot, on the other foot, again, and again, and again.

You must not fall.

When you lose your balance, resist for a long time before turning yourself toward the earth. Then jump.

You must not force yourself to stay steady. You must move forward.

You must win.

The wire trembles. The tendency is to want to calm it by force. In fact, you must move with grace and suppleness to avoid disturbing the song of the cable.

It is better to take your first steps without a balancing pole. Above all, it is natural. This cumbersome bar can help an experienced walker to make an effortless crossing, but it is utterly useless to the beginner. You should not begin to think about a balancing pole until you have mastered balancing on one foot and have been able to make a partial crossing without losing your composure.

The balancing pole is generally a wooden rod or a metal tube with a diameter that allows for easy handling; it is five to eight meters in length. Its weight varies according to the situation: the exercise balancing pole weighs twenty pounds; the balancing pole used in great crossings can be as heavy as fifty pounds. The way it is made is the wire walker's secret. Assemble your own and do not tell anyone how you did it.

So that the foot will feel the cable and not lend itself to accidental slips, buffalo-hide slippers are recommended, though in rainy weather these should be replaced by slippers with rubber soles. But any unreinforced shoes with the main sole removed, or even thick socks—several on each foot—will do the job quite well. In the same way, a twisted green branch or an old rusty pipe will be perfectly adequate for the first balancing pole.

Don't waste your time on the ground.

Work without stopping. Little by little, the wire must belong to you.

Hold the balancing pole firmly, arms spread. Never dip it. It is moved to the left, to the right, in a horizontal gesture. The body does not lean. The hips do not move. The leg is rigid without being dead. But you discover that on your own.

By the end of the day, you will have made your first crossing.

WALKING

The horseman knows the pleasure of working his horse at a slow pace. He leaves galloping to the frenzied knight.

Perfectly calm, the high-wire walker will endlessly practice "the Time of the Rope." This consists of traveling the length of his cable slowly, one step at a time. This is the first exercise with the balancing pole. It is also the most important and the most ancient. After a great number of crossings back and forth, you will know what it is to go and what it is to return. Continue to do this for a long time before attempting a real walk. For a walk on the wire must be slow and careful, like a line pulled tight by the strength of your eyes: the body straight, the foot firmly inside the wire with each step, the balancing pole motionless.

To put your whole foot on the wire all at once produces a sure though heavy kind of walking, but if you first slide your toes, then your sole, and finally your heel onto the wire, you will be able to experience the intoxicating lightness that is so magnificent at great heights. And then people will say of you: "He is strolling on his wire!" Dismount and pace off nine meters holding the balancing pole: that is the perfect walk! This test is necessary: you were beginning to feel like a high-wire walker.

Walking is the soul of the wire. There are an infinite number of styles.

There is the walk that glides, like that of a bullfighter who slowly approaches his adversary, the presence of danger growing with each new step, his body arched outrageously, hypnotized.

There is the unbroken, continuous walk, without the least concern for balance, the pole on your shoulder, your arm swinging and your eyes turned upward, as if you were looking for your thoughts in the sky; this is the solid walk of a man of the earth returning home, a tool over his shoulder, satisfied with his day's work.

These walks happen to be mine.

Discover your own. Work on them until they are perfect.

RUNNING

Running?
   Ah! Yes, running is entertaining.
   It's fresh, it's tempting, it's joyous, it's distracting.
   All running is joyful.
   Ah! How he runs on his wire!

You are running to a certain fall.

Running will come naturally from a light and rapid way of walking.
   Let it come by itself.

When you walk, the foot follows the line of the wire: in this way you can do extremely rapid crossings and brief runs. But to run vigorously on a cable, you must put your feet sideways across the wire, like a duck. To begin, run on the wire thinking only of regularity; running will be difficult. Add speed, and it will become impossible.
   You must set your eyes so that they take in the whole length of the wire. You must feel it in space. Measure its extension. The distance is too great to hazard without courage: hold the balancing pole in front of you and take off with a sure and straight step. With the help of your open arms, clear a path for yourself, push your hips along the wire to the very end; your feet will follow, your body will get through. You want your steps to control this length of steel. Launch yourself then, and cross it with three long strides.

To understand running is to harmonize the wind of your steps with the breath of the wire—without asking questions.

Running is not the way to go quickly from one end of the wire to the other.

Running? It's the acrobat's laughter!

THE QUEST FOR IMMOBILITY

This is the mystery of the rope dance. The essence, the secret. Time plays no part in achieving it.

Or perhaps I should say "in approaching it."

To approach it, the high-wire walker turns himself into an alchemist. Again and again, he attempts it along the wire, but without ever entering the Domain of Immobility—where, I was told, the arms become useless, hanging alongside a body that is ten times heavier than before.

The feeling of a second of immobility—if the wire grants it to you—is an intimate happiness.

Come to the middle of the wire with the most beautiful of your walks.

Achieve a state of balance, and then wait. All by itself, the balancing pole will become horizontal, your body will settle on two fixed and solid legs. Immobility will come promptly. Or so you would think.

You will feel yourself immobile: I'm not moving, therefore I'm immobile.

And what about your eyes that watch and wander?

I saw your eyes climbing up through the trees.

And those thoughts in your skull, stammering back and forth?

And the blood rushing through your veins? And the wind in your hair? And the bobbing wire? And all this air you eat and chew?

What a racket!

No, the tiny inhabitants of the weeds have never seen such an agitated being.

The quest for immobility is even more deceptive if you give up the balancing pole, but it is absolutely essential.

You must devote yourself to it.

Balanced on one foot, the balancing foot, slowly bring your arm and leg to rest. Hold this position. This is the first point. Then put your free leg into contact with the other, your two feet on the wire; your arms will serve as a balancing pole, you will gradually move them less and less. This is the second point. Now you must get rid of these arms: by crossing them in front of you, by letting them hang naturally, or by putting them behind your back. All this happens in surreptitious ways. Clandestinely. This is the third point.

It is now a matter of patience. It is between the wire and you.

Approach. Feel how balance no longer exists. Be on the lookout for the moment when you will suddenly stop breathing. An otherworldly heaviness will anchor you to the cable. You will breathe along it: the air will surge from the end of the wire, work its way slowly along it, pierce the soles of your feet, climb up through your legs, inundate your body, and in the end reach your nostrils. You will exhale without any pause, and your breath will travel back along the same path: softly, from your lips, you will expel the air, and it will go down, flow around each muscle, trace the outline of your feet, and then reenter the wire. . . .

Do not abandon your breath halfway. Pursue it until it escapes through the end of your wire, in the same way it came.

Your breathing will become slow, distended, long like a thread.

You and the rigging will become a single body, solid as a rock.

You will feel yourself a thing of balance. You will become wire.

Once you have built this flawless balance, so fleeting and fragile, it will be as dense for you as granite.

If no thought came to disturb this miracle, it would go on and on. But man, who is astonished by everything, himself included, quickly loses hold of it.

The minute point of balance hovers above the wire, knocks against the wire walker, and navigates like a feather in the wind of his efforts.

Let this wind slacken, let it die, and the feather will soon enter the wire walker and come to rest in his center of gravity.

This is the way it happens then: first, you reach a relative calm; then, you achieve a second, finer balance; and finally, if only rarely, you attain a brief instant of absolute immobility.

For the wind of our thoughts is more violent than the wind of balance and will soon set this delicate feather fluttering again.

BAREFOOT

I am nostalgic for the old ropes.

You walked on them with bare feet. Not so on the cable.

How proud the tightrope walker was. On the bottom of each foot there was an astonishing tattoo, a mark made far above the crowds. It was the sign of his art and his daring, and only he knew it was there. Its hardness was proof to him that he was Emperor of the Air, and even on the ground he continued to walk on these tough, callused lines.

The foot lived well when it lived with hemp.

The steel cable has replaced the rope, and if it breathes it is only because its soul is made of hemp. And even though the foot can never merge with the metal, you must go back often to working barefoot. This is indispensable. The foot can then find its place on the cable, and the cable can find its place in the foot.

But that must be attempted delicately.

The wire penetrates between the big toe and the second toe, crosses the foot along the whole length of the sole, and escapes behind the middle of the heel. One can also make the wire enter along the bottom of the big toe; the sole is then traversed obliquely, and the cable leaves slightly to one side of the heel. If this second method is acceptable for certain walks, the first is nevertheless essential. You must be able to use the big toe and the second toe to grip the wire and hang on to it (this is the only way to avoid a slip during a Death Walk).

Remain balanced on one foot until the pain is no longer bearable, and then prolong this suffering for another minute before changing feet.

Repeat the exercise, then attempt a series of walks. Wait until the foot is perfectly placed before taking the next step.

When the positioning of each foot has become quite natural, the legs will have gained their independence, and your step will have become noble and sure.

You won't get results from a few hours of serious work. You must continue until your flesh understands it.

But I promise that when your feet slide to rest on a cable bed, you will astonish yourself with a smile of deep weariness.

Look: on your sole there is what my friend Fouad calls the Line of Laughter. It corresponds to the mark of the wire.

THE HIGH-WIRE WALKER'S SALUTE

Before entering the last phase of combat,
the bullfighter removes his montera
and, in a neat circling gesture, presents it to the crowd.
Then he throws it onto the sand.
The matador's salute is a dedication.

When the balloon is ready, the pilot orders: "Hands off!"
Rising above a forest of arms, he flourishes his cap
in broad figure eights and disappears.
The aeronaut's salute is a farewell.

The wire walker, after setting foot on the cable,
walks halfway across, stops, and slides down to one knee.
He removes one hand from his balancing pole.
The wire walker's salute is a dedication.
Of strength, of magnificence.
He thrusts his fist into the teeth of the wind,
and in the same movement his fist opens to receive the answer.
The wire walker reads it in his own hand, there, resting
on one knee, in the middle of the wire.
News of death, a promise of joy:
he lets nothing escape
of what he has learned.

*

Except for the Time of the Rope, the Salute is the first exercise the high-wire walker must learn.

There is the standing salute, the kneeling salute, and the sitting salute.

The first is made on one leg, balancing pole resting horizontally on the raised thigh, the arm up.

The second is the true high-wire walker's salute. So that it will be perfect, a part of the body's weight must rest on the top of the foot where it joins the ankle, and the whole top of the foot must be touching the cable—not just the knuckles of the foot. You often see this, and it is a disgrace.

The sitting salute is the same as the standing, except that the wire passes under the thigh and the middle of the buttocks.

You can achieve the sitting salute unexpectedly—by jumping onto the wire from the standing position. The leg muscles will absorb the vibrations of this sudden encounter with the cable.

There are numerous variations to the high-wire walker's salute.

I have discovered old engravings in which the acrobat is kneeling, but only the knee is touching the rope; the rest of the leg is in the air perpendicular to the wire.

A salute is made when you step onto the wire, but there is also the salute that concludes a performance, and as a general rule the strongest moment of any exercise can be accompanied by an appropriate salute. There is no particular salute without a balancing pole. One possibility would be to imitate those gymnasts with big mustaches who posed for the earliest cameras: standing proudly and simply, arms crossed, head held high, feet almost at right angles, the torso inflated. I do this. I call it the Salute in the Old Style.

But there is nothing, it seems to me, more gravely majestic than the moment when the high-wire walker, with admirable reverence, takes leave of his wire.

EXERCISES

Walking, running, and the salute precede a multitude of exercises; an infinite number, in fact, if one were to include all the variants. Often the balancing pole is required; sometimes special equipment must be used. One must also mention the net, the belt, and other safety systems. They guarantee the conquest of the impossible—but at the same time they cheapen the victory. A rule of thumb would be the following: anything that can be done on the ground can be done on the wire, although sometimes necessarily in a slightly different form. To draw up the complete list of exercises for rope, cable, and low wire would be as impossible as pretending to draw up a list of newly invented exercises, exercises that have not yet been done, or exercises that are unheard of, that defy execution.

Here, in any case, is a list—presented more or less in order of appearance:

The Time of the Rope. Walking.
Running.
The salute.
Dancing.
Splits.
The pretend fall.
The headstand (with or without balancing pole).
Resting on the wire, in a supine position.
The genuflection; walking while genuflecting.
Balancing on one knee.
The planche: balancing on one leg.
One-arm handstand.

The cartwheel.

Balancing, facing the audience.

High-bar exercises.

Descending an inclined cable by sliding on the stomach (a specialty of the Middle Ages); hanging from the back of the neck, or with one foot attached to a pulley.

The Death Walk (up or down an inclined cable, with or without the balancing pole).

Blindfolded: walking with the head covered, walking in a sack.

Dancing in wooden shoes.

Dancing with scythes, sickles, or daggers attached to the ankles.

Walking with feet in baskets (with wicker bottoms or fake bottoms made of cloth).

The bound walk: ankles chained together.

Jumping through a paper hoop.

Walking with a pennant, crossing with flags.

With a pitcher and glass of water: refreshments on the rope.

Walking with a candlestick or sword (the prop is balanced on the chin, the nose, or even the forehead, for the length of a balancing or, for wire walkers of great heights, for the length of a crossing with the balancing pole—without the balancing pole for slack-rope walkers).

Tricks with a Chinese umbrella or an Indian fan (often on an inclined rope).

The half-turn without the balancing pole.

The half-turn jump without the balancing pole.

The half-turn with the balancing pole (the wire walker turns; his balancing pole does not move).

Juggling (usually with balls, clubs, torches, or hoops), with or without the balancing pole. The pole can be balanced off-center on the wire with the help of the balancing foot.

Walking in a hoop. (The hoop rolls on the wire and is kept in a vertical position by the feet of the wire walker, who walks on the inside.)

Hoop around the ankles. (The hoop is kept in a horizontal position by the ankles, which means the wire walker must take broad, semicircular steps so as not to lose the hoop.)

Passing a hoop over the body and stepping out.

Walking with the balancing pole behind the back.

Walking with the balancing pole above the head, arms fully extended.

With the balancing pole on the shoulders.

Putting the balancing pole behind the back (over the shoulders or under the legs).

Walking backward.

Wearing disguises.

Imitating characters, animals.

Wearing armor.

Doing comedy routines on the wire.

Playing a musical instrument (in all positions).

Balancing on a small wooden plank (motionless, or with tiny leaps forward).

Balancing on a ladder, or on a step ladder.

Balancing on a chair, its struts or legs resting on the rope.

With a table and chair: a meal on the wire.

With a stove and kitchen equipment: cooking an omelette on the wire.

Pistol dancing, sword dancing. Knife throwing.

Precision shooting on the wire, shooting at a moving target, shooting balloons.

On a velocipede, bicycle.

On a unicycle (regular-size, giant).

Walking on stilts.

High jumping. Hurdling a table.

Jumping rope. Double, triple, crisscross, while moving forward.

Jumping over a riding crop held in both hands, frontward and backward.

High-wire walker's somersault (forward roll with jump start with a balancing pole).

True somersault (feet to feet), frontward or backward (the principle exercise of low-wire artists and ropedancers, but unthinkable for a wire walker of great heights without protection).

The caboulot (backward roll with a balancing pole). Crossing the wire with caboulots.

The reverse (a caboulot without the balancing pole in which the acrobat takes hold of the cable behind him from a lying position and pulls, which rolls him over backward and puts him in a sitting position).

The human load (carrying someone on your back); the "baptism of wire" (taking someone from the audience and putting him on the wire for the first time); pushing a wheelbarrow with someone in it.

Falling astride the wire (usually to initiate a series of caboulots).

Spinning around the wire, starting from a straddling position.

Balancing a perch on the forehead, with crossing.

Hanging: from the knees, ankles, or toes.

Tightrope acts on a slack wire attached below the main cable.

The high-bar catch-and-swing. (After a real or feigned slip, the wire walker, hanging by his hands, gets back onto the wire by flaring out his legs over it; as soon as his feet catch hold of the wire, he turns around it, before springing to a standing position.)

Fireworks shot off on the wire (knapsack filled with sand in which fuses have been planted; helmet with a pinwheel; balancing pole

adorned with flares and catherine wheels—lighted with a cigarette at the middle of the wire). This exercise is often fatal.

Jumping on one foot, with crossing.

Crossing a burning wire (with boots and asbestos clothes).

"True" crossing on a motorcycle (holding the balancing pole, with
no counterweight under the machine).

"False" crossing on a motorcycle (with a trapeze that works as a
counterweight and holds the machine on the cable).

Exercises with a partner, group exercises:

The human column, either stationary or advancing along the wire
(two, three, or four people on the shoulders of the under-stander).

The human column on a unicycle, on a bicycle (with two or three
people).

The bicycle with trapeze hanging below the wheels (one or two
trapezes).

The human pyramid (metal bars—"forks"—create a scaffolding
for three, four, five, six, seven, eight, or nine people).

A pyramid of three bicycles, with crossing.

Two people passing each other from opposite directions, without a
balancing pole, by "ducking" (without touching), by "embracing" (grabbing the partners' hands and turning while leaning
outward).

Passing the sleeper. (You cross your partner, who is lying down on
the cable, by placing your foot on his stomach.)

Passing the sleeper by jumping over him.

Jumping over the seated partner.

Passing with a balancing pole (with the partner seated, or lying
down).

Climbing on the partner's back, then shoulders, and leaping forward, to land feet first on the wire.

Backward somersault (*salto mortale*) from the shoulders of an
under-stander to the shoulders of another (never done without
a safety belt).

Jumping from a springboard or teeterboard attached to the cable
and landing on the under-stander's shoulders.

The Ladder of Death. (In the beginning, a simple ladder was placed
flat across the wire, with one acrobat at each end. Today, the
ladder is solidly attached to the cable and can freely pivot
around it.)

The human belt. (The body of the rider is wrapped around the
waist of the under-stander.)

The human wheelbarrow. (The rider has his legs attached to the
waist of the carrier and holds a wheel in his hands that he guides
along the wire.)

Head to head.

Head to foot. (The top mounter stands on the under-stander's head.)

The wire walker's somersault (forward caboulot) over one, two,
three, or four people.

Working with several wires at different heights and angles.

Working with a wire that changes heights and angles during the act.

Working with animals as partners (bears, monkeys, birds).

It is also important to mention the roles of the various kinds of
wires:

There are exercises for low-wire artists and ropedancers that
cannot be done on a high-wire walker's cable; others can be done
on any kind of wire. It is obvious that an acrobat on a slack rope
one and a half meters from the ground can raise his eyes for a long
time to keep an object balanced on his forehead or to juggle; the
high-wire walker, on a cable without elasticity or movement, can

do no more than attempt the same exercise without a balancing pole. He will never succeed, however, unless he has immense talent.

The high-wire walker must be an inventor.

Jean-Francois Gravelet, a.k.a. Charles Blondin, prepared an omelette on the wire; he also opened a bottle of champagne and toasted the crowd. He even managed to take photographs—from the middle of the wire—of the crowd that was watching him cross the rapids at Niagara Falls.

Madame Saqui created historical frescoes to the glory of Emperor Napoleon, all by herself on the tightrope.

Rudy Omankowsky, Jr., set off numerous fireworks from his cable. He specialized in somersaulting from a bicycle over four people (the bike would fall into the net at the moment of takeoff). His father, "Papa Rudy" Omankowsky, taught him the extraordinary dismount from the giant unicycle: jumping forward onto the cable. He himself was the master of a series of caboulots—his legs now shooting out to the right, now to the left, now on either side of the wire—and performed a dramatic crossing in a sack that ended with straddle falls and a series of rolls.

The ventriloquist Señor Wences has told me that on the tightrope, "facing the audience," Miguel Robledillo imitated a staggering drunk.

Francis Brunn, the legendary juggler, remembers admiringly how Alzana would jump rope on wet cables and continue to jump even after he had lost balance and was being carried away from the axis of the wire.

I myself have witnessed the delicate crossings of Sharif Magomiedoff several times: he places the tip of his wife's foot on his forehead and walks along the wire while keeping her balanced—she herself is protected from falling by a safety belt. My friend Pedro Carillo goes down the steepest walk by jumping without a balancing pole and, almost in total darkness, slides down—sometimes backward—to reach the ground.

As for myself, I am endlessly hunting for new exercises—like throwing away the balancing pole; the half-turn with balancing pole sweeping through space; walking on tiptoe so as not to wake up the sleeping circus; bouncing a ball on my forehead; and other juggling acts directly inspired by Francis Brunn.

And, lest I forget the masters of us all: the high-wire animals. Artists have painted them with great enthusiasm, and photographs have allowed us to know the truth that lurks behind the legends.

*

Walking in wicker baskets is an old and very pleasant exercise. A great family of wire walkers robbed a cigarette manufacturer in this way.

It all happened long ago, so perhaps the story can now be told.

Once, while performing outdoors, they attached one end of their rope to the window of a cigarette warehouse. Having come to the basket exercise in their performance, the wire walkers repeated it so many times that the audience, which did not share this excessive passion for baskets, began to hoot with impatience.

The baskets were being systematically loaded at one end of the wire and then carefully emptied at the other. In this way, the family managed to steal enough cigarettes to fill a hay cart.

WITHOUT A BALANCING POLE

This is the foundation of the art of high-wire walking.

For safety reasons, however, the high-wire walker has forgotten it.

It is rare to see a high-wire walker at great heights without a balancing pole.

It is, however, the purest image of a man on a line.

In a crossing without balancing pole, we see the qualities of an acrobat; in a true performance without balancing pole, we salute the blood of the high-wire walker.

The succession of balancings—first on one foot and then on the other—that allowed you to move along the wire with skill must now be developed into a controlled walk. The crossing must be made at an even speed, without the slightest loss of equilibrium.

If before you had to fix your eyes on the cable several yards in front of you, now you must look all the way to the end. This connection with the "target" is obligatory, and more than once it has saved a life.

Running without a balancing pole can be attempted only after your walk has become infallible. You can master it with constant and devoted work over a number of years. Like a juggler, you must practice fiercely and without distraction. Otherwise, your attempts on the wire will remain attempts, and you will always lose.

For example, consider the half-turn:

You can have an exact idea of it without ever being able to do it successfully.

Create a vertical motion in the wire; the moment to attempt the half-turn is when the wave is at its maximum height; the body will be lighter, the feet will turn more easily. This wave is imperceptible. Press down harder with the back foot; it will serve as a pivot. Remember that the feet never completely leave the wire during a half-turn.

To turn around on both legs at once, you must raise yourself slightly on the balls of your feet; the heels swivel one hundred and eighty degrees to meet up with the wire again at the same time as the front part of your feet. The half-turn can be done to the right or the left, after coming to a full stop or in the middle of a walk. This last will come as a surprise—like a sleepwalker suddenly changing direction.

If I had to present myself in the Paradise of Rope Dancers by doing one walk, and one walk only, I would make my entrance without a balancing pole. I would walk as naturally as possible, my arms at my sides, letting them sway slightly to the rhythm of my step. I would walk straight ahead without thinking for a single moment that I was on a wire: like some passerby receding into the distance.

And my salute would be a one-knee balancing without pole— which I believe is something no one has ever done before.

THE KING POLES

The high-wire walker no longer lives among the low branches of the trees. A new wire is waiting for him.

A solid gray wire, perhaps fifteen meters long, stretched out six or eight meters above the ground between two poles painted in the performer's favorite color. On these poles the wire walker can rest, place his different balancing poles, store his chair or his bicycle, as well as his juggling clubs and unicycle. The platform floor should be a square of wood strong enough to support all the equipment and the aerialist himself. It is positioned below the cable. The platforms of low-wire artists and ropedancers are positioned above the cable. They step down onto their cable. The high-wire walker, however, steps up onto his. Along the vertical axis of the walk cable, and on each side, an ungreased cable is stretched down to the ground. One of these inclined cables is drawn out to maximum length for the Death Walk. It is along this path that you will climb up to the installation, unless you have the patience to build a hemp-rope ladder with oak rungs.

Each pole is held vertically by the "obseclungs"—two thin cables attached to the top of the pole that come down perpendicular to the walk line and form a forty-five-degree angle with the ground. These guy wires are pulled into place by pulleys attached with "beckets" to "stakes." The whole installation is thus anchored by the stakes, thick steel bars—formerly wooden bars—that are driven into the ground with sledgehammers. These in turn have a sling of steel or hemp attached to them. This is called the becket.

Putting up the king poles will be your first great joy as a high-wire walker.

You measure the terrain. In the designated spots you lay out the pole sections that you will later fit together; these are hollow tubes or trussed pylons. Then you proceed to the "dressing": one by one jibing the platforms and poles with all their cables, in an order so complicated that the neophyte will have to go through it several times before he can assume sole responsibility for it. It goes without saying that you must have won the friendship of an old high-wire walker who will share his rigging secrets with you, and that he is with you now. If not, you will have to go about it according to your own ideas, and sooner or later you will pay for it with your life.

When the equipment is ready, you drive in the stakes. If five men produce a series of strokes in rapid succession—"a flying five"—watch out for the pieces of steel that whistle down, to land in a tree trunk twenty feet away, or in the flesh of a man who was not paying attention.

You raise up the king poles. One after the other. With the aid of a six-sheave block and tackle. Then you attach the tightening device: a heavy chain hoist or a giant turnbuckle. This latter should not be used for a big installation if the longitudinal section of the screw forms a series of triangles, for it wears out and gives way. The screw should have a square shape so that it will never loosen. This is the kind of turnbuckle used for coupling railroad cars.

The curvature of the wire changes according to the height. Soon it will trace a straight line that seems rigorous; you then attach the cavalletti to the blocks and give a final turn to the tightening device— the "pull to death"—just before beginning your work.

To give your routines on the wire an aspect of perfection and to execute highly delicate balancings, the cable must not buckle or sway between the two poles. To avoid this, you attach a thin plate of light metal over the walk cable at appropriate intervals. These plates will fit snugly over the wire. To each flap you attach a length of hemp, the same thickness as the walk cable, that will be drawn down to the ground from various points on the wire at the same angle as the obseclungs. These are the cavallettis. The shape of the plates allows a bicycle rim to pass over them without jumping off track; because of the thickness of the ropes that secure them, you will not find yourself on the ground looking at your own severed arm after an accidental slip—which happened to an artist who had chosen to use a thin steel wire.

At times the cavallettis require these plates; at other times they do not. The cavallettis are necessary for great crossings and preferable for "high work" between the poles; in the open air, they are generally spaced fifteen meters apart. But Blondin, who worked on rope, placed them at every two meters for difficult crossings.

For a fifteen-meter wire between two poles, two cavallettis will be acceptable. Obviously, when there are too many cavallettis or when they are too close to one another, we sense the amateurism and cowardice of the performer. If you want to avoid the slightest jolt on the cable, if you want to be certain that it will not vibrate as you go over the cavallettis, at the end of each rope you must use a pulley and attach a counterweight—a bag of sand or a bucket of water. The rope crosses through the pulley, which is attached two meters from the ground by a brace anchored to a chain that in turn is tied to a stake. The wire will then breathe with each of your steps without giving way or turning.

All this must be learned. You cannot make it up.

There are some high-wire walkers who would rather die with their knowledge than let newcomers learn it. Besides, circus people distrust anyone who does not "live on the road," and how could it be otherwise?

The length of the walk cable should always exceed ten meters;

the length works as a function of the height of the poles. For six-meter poles, a good length is twelve meters. A number of aerialists would say fifteen meters; this makes the installation easier, since the circus ring measures thirteen and a half meters in diameter and the poles are always placed just outside the ring. The more one stretches the line without raising the height, the lower the installation will seem. And vice versa.

The high-wire walker eagerly carries his balancing pole to the foot of the king poles. With a smile he abandons the "little wire" of his first crossings. From now on, he will return to it only to learn new exercises or to throw himself into some whirling caper he hopes to invent. He puts his foot on the inclined cable and scales the sky, where the motionless birds are waiting to meet him.

ALONE ON HIS WIRE

Up above, about to begin a long acquaintance with his new territory, the high-wire walker feels himself alone. His body will remain motionless for a long time. Grasping the platform with both hands behind him, he stands before the cable, as if he did not dare set foot on it.

It looks as though he is idly basking in the setting sun.

Not at all. He is buying time.

He measures space, feels out the void, weighs distances, watches over the state of things, takes in the position of each object around him. Trembling, he savors his solitude. He knows that if he makes it across, he will be a high-wire walker.

He wants to line up his doubts and fears with his thoughts—in order to hoist up the courage he has left.

But that takes too much time.

The cable grows longer, the sky becomes dark, the other platform is now a hundred meters away. The ground is no longer in the same place; it has moved even lower. Cries come from the woods. The end of the day is near.

At the deepest moment of his despair, feeling he must now give up, the high-wire walker grabs his balancing pole and moves forward. Step by step, he crosses over.

This is his first accomplishment.

He stands there trying to absorb it, his eyes blankly staring at this new platform, while darkness skims over the ground.

With the tops of the trees he shares the day's last light, a light softer than air.

Alone on his wire, he wraps himself more deeply in a wild and scathing happiness, crossing helter-skelter into the dampness of the evening. He attaches his balancing pole to the platform before settling down at the top of the mast. There, in a corner of dark and chilly space, he waits calmly for the night to come.

PRACTICE

The shock of it lasted several days.

Every morning he ran to his wire, leaping over the grass so the dew would not weigh him down. Distracted by so much happiness, he would let himself simply walk back and forth, again and again. There are those who think this coming and going will turn them into high-wire walkers. The true man of the wire, however, cannot accept this horizontal monotony for very long: he knows that the path he is about to take has no limit. In remembrance of his recent birth, he stops short and sets to work. Silent and alone, he brings to the high cable everything he has learned down below. He discards the movements space will not support and gathers up the others into a group that he will polish, refine, lighten, and bring closer and closer to himself.

Each day he adds another mastered element.

Soon he goes out on his wire with only one goal: to discover new ideas, to invent a combination of unexpected gestures. He goes out hunting. And what he catches he hangs on his wire. Then he distracts himself with inconsequential walks, whimsical postures, exercises with no future, like a bear wallowing in his pool at the zoo. And if he loses his taste for movement to such an extent that he loses control, better that he should rest on the wire than stop and climb down. For you must reach some apex before stepping to the ground, no matter how small it is: your existence as a high-wire walker is at stake. You must leave the wire in triumph, not out of weariness.

Now that he knows how to go about practicing, each session will be longer, more fruitful, and the day will be meaningless unless it bears the shape of the wire.

Then the music starts!

For stimulation, he turns on the brassiest Circassian marches; he draws courage from Spanish bullfighting music; and, with exquisite ardor, he surrounds himself with the sound of a full orchestra.

THE WIRE WALKER AT REST

At the time when wire walkers stretched their ropes between two X's of wood, one of the X's was always reserved for resting.

There was a simple hemp line stretched between the tops of the two beams, high enough for the dancer to lean the small of his back against it. It was covered by a large cloth decorated in the artist's colors and embroidered with fine gold threads. Leaning against it in this way, the acrobat could indifferently let his eyes wander down to settle on the rope.

As his name indicates, the wire walker of great heights is a dreamer: he has another way of resting. He stretches out on his cable and contemplates the sky. There he gathers his strength, recovers the serenity he may have lost, regains his courage and his faith. But weariness is necessary: you must not treat resting as an exercise.

Sit down. Fold one leg on the cable and then lean backward until your head touches it. A moment later the foot will begin to slide, and the leg will stretch out completely; the other leg will hang down and sway. Sometimes one hand lets go of the pole; sometimes it retrieves it. You want to feel the line of the wire. It will become your spinal column. Each passing second shrieks like a grindstone. An endless pain takes hold of your body and breaks it down muscle by muscle. If you resist and cross the threshold of what is bearable, the torture will extend into your bones and break them one by one across the wire. You will be a skeleton balanced on a razor blade. Beyond this limit, millions of terrifying enchantments await you. Beyond this limit, breath and confidence go together. And still further beyond, a patience without desire will give each of your thoughts its real density.

Then be lazy—to the point of delirium!

With your back on the wire, you feel the vastness of the sky. To be a wire walker in its profoundest sense means to leave the wire behind you, to discover the cables that have been strung even higher and, step by step, to reach the Magic Wire of Immobility, the Wire that belongs to the Masters of the World. The earth itself rests on it. It is the Wire that links the finite to the infinite: the straightest, shortest path between one star and the next.

Now close your eyes.

The cable is limpid. Your body is silent. Together, they are motionless. Only your leg quivers. You would like to cut it off, to turn your body into a single human wire. But already it no longer belongs to you, is no longer a part of you. Like the chess player who closes his eyes and sees a whole plain of black and white squares passing under his feet, you close your eyes and see only a magnificent gray wire.

The silent wind of your eyes inhabits it.

A silence invaded by light.

Penetrate this luminosity by seeking out its source. Plunge down to find the place where nothing breathes, into the blackness that is hidden inside it. Keep going until you reach the other side of the light. It is a dazzling clarity, a clamorous splendor: wet, whirling, often colorless. As if through a black mirror, you will see a gleaming, untouched wire. That is the image you are looking for. It will quickly be jumbled together with the fireworks of new impressions. Once this image has come, however, the high-wire walker can live in space. For whole hours, for portions of entire days, as if time had come to a halt. No one else will ever notice.

You must throw yourself into this meaningless search for rest—without hoping for a result.

Here is the wire walker stretched out on his gigantic antenna, listening to the world. He can feel the noise of the city rise up to him; he can distinguish among the thousand sounds that fill the silence of the countryside. He starts at the whistling of shooting stars.

And all that puts him to sleep.

A deep breathing invades him.

Each time he draws in his breath, he hears noises; each time he exhales, he hears nothing. Then, during the space of several heartbeats, he forgets everything. He begins to snore. But between his sighs, what silence!

Below him, nothing. Neither dogs nor people. Nature has gone to sleep as well, so that the wire walker, balanced on his huge tuning fork, can at last begin to dream.

THE BLINDFOLDED DEATH WALK

You have no idea what's in store for you.

A cable inclined at a thirty-degree angle. From the ground to the top of the pole or the church bell tower. Three hundred meters. Guy-lined at intervals by a few lengths of hemp. Swaying in the face of a drowsing sun.

Despite all the care that has been given to its installation, the wire will never demark an evenly ascending line. It will dip into space, become horizontal at low altitudes, gently raise its head, lift up its nose, and with growing malice mime a venomous verticality in its last section.

When a blindfolded Death Walk takes place, it is always announced as an "attempt."

Step by step you will climb up, your eyes pressed against the black cloth, your face buried in the suffocating sack. Blind, deaf, and dumb, you will doubt you can reach the end of the wire.

The sun, which has been beating down since dawn, has drawn out the grease hidden in the soul of the cable. With your first steps, the whole installation will begin to move. Each cavalletti will pull on its area—which will amplify the wire's oscillation, as if it were now trying to throw you off. Without ever knowing where they are, your feet will unexpectedly touch an oily spot—and you will advance by millimeters, your hands clutching the balancing pole. The one you have chosen is long and heavy, and with each step forward it will grow even heavier. You will be at the end of your strength when the abrupt angle of the last steps begins, and the wind will be waiting in ambush for you there. You will think you are in the middle of the wire, so you will kneel down for an impeccable aerialist's salute, which will be ridiculous, for in fact you will be only ten meters from your starting point. You will lengthen your strides with the thought that you are half finished with the crossing, and you will bang your body into the pole or a stone of the building, for the walk is over. Then, with a superb gesture, you will tear off the blindfold and the hood, almost falling with the last step, for your vertigo will be total as you stand in the sudden dazzling light of the sun.

The first ascent will remain the most vivid sensation in your life as a high-wire walker. You will think: My shadow was faithful, it has led me this far, and if by chance courage fails me, I will throw the corpse of my memories helter-skelter on the wire, and in this way reach the heart of a storm that will allow me to scale these ferocious heights.

FAKES

I know a man who sells himself body and soul to the highest bidder.

He uses a blindfold with holes in it, an immense balancing pole that hangs over both sides of his overly guy-lined wire, and presents his exercises above a net. He has learned how to walk on the cable with an "extension cord"—a second wire that runs parallel to the one he walks on. It is just above his head, and he can grab onto it whenever he wants.

Over the circus rings where he works as a so-called high-wire walker, he uses a "mechanic." This is an almost invisible cable attached to a safety belt that has been sewn into his costume. His assistant, who stays on the ground during his performance, manipulates the string with tiny, discrete movements, as though he were controlling a puppet. As a result, this equilibrist is able to do stunts that no wire walker could ever attempt, much less accomplish. Three times I saw him do a backward somersault on an inclined wire: this is impossible. Three times I saw him fail to gain his footing. Three times I saw his body fall to one side of the wire— although this was imperceptible to the crowd—and three times I saw his balance righted by the safety line. The rest of his performance was punctuated by cries, feigned slips, and pretend falls. From the simplest, most limpid exercises he knew how to extract interminable difficulties, which he mimed in the most grotesque fashion. Before he stepped onto the wire, he would take great care to rub the soles of his shoes with resin powder. Thus, his feet were not placed on the wire, they were glued to it. When I had the chance to walk on his wire, I could not take a step: my feet got stuck. I am used to wearing old and extremely smooth slippers so my walks will be as lithe and graceful as possible.

The terrain of the high-wire walker is bounded by death, not by props. And when a wire walker inspires pity, he deserves death ten times over.

Anyone can use a net, an extension cord, a blindfold with holes in it, a trick balancing pole, resin, cavallettis that touch each other, and a mechanic. To make life even sweeter for these people, I would advise them to practice falling as well. In the realm of the Absurd, they would become the masters of every artifice.

True high-wire walkers do not do such things.

But I know another aerialist.

He often appears on the wire of my dreams.

He is immense in his red-and-black cape—which he throws down to the crowd with a giant's laughter following his first crossing. At times he is majestic. He does the simplest exercises, even the ones that other artists disdain. But he performs them with such finesse, such cunning and ease, that everything about them seems difficult. At other times, he acts like a clown, makes false steps, tangles his feet, and stops in the middle of a move to strike a comic, ridiculous pose. At still other times, he is wild, throwing himself into mad stunts without even trying to succeed. He attacks the wire, slips, catches himself, bangs his head and howls, foams, springs back.

He is alone, like a flame, and the music of his blood silences all our cheers.

But he can hear what the people in the first row are whispering:

"Isn't he charming?"

"Do you think he's going to fly?"

Murderers!

At that point, he wipes off his sweat with the back of his arm and spits into the arena.

The customer is always right!

With dash and daring he responds disdainfully by pretending to slip with each step, stunning the many spectators who have no idea what he is doing. Then he reaches his platform with classic grace, the perfection he can achieve whenever he wants to.

Laughing, I stand up to applaud him.

I allow him everything. Whatever he does I will accept.

And if he would like to start working with a net, well, maybe I wouldn't disapprove.

THE PERFORMANCE

As the days went on, I found that I could repeat the same steps, the same movements.

My work was becoming serious.

I would begin with several crossings "to build confidence." But I was eager to get to what I love to do best: the slowest walks; the simplest, most delicate routines.

It was in a meadow at the end of a day of hard training that I found my first spectator, who had no doubt been attracted by my silence.

Before leaving the wire, I had allowed myself to do a crossing with one foot dragging behind me, thinking of all the things that foot might be able to do.

Suddenly, the tall hedge behind me opened.

A huge cow's head had just placed itself noiselessly on a row of brambles, its muzzle calm, its eye friendly.

Bashful at being surprised during my exercises, I withdrew very softly to the platform and then set out straight and erect to the middle of the cable, where I performed a mathematically exact half-turn and kneeled to my visitor in the most perfect fashion.

I continued to do the best and most beautiful things I knew. I did the exercises in the order I had prepared them during my practice sessions; I added what a man of the wire thinks he possesses: the expansiveness of movement, the steadiness of eye, the feeling of victory, the humor of gestures. I climbed down from the wire, covered with sweat, unable to remember having once taken a breath, while the enormous animal turned around, chewing slowly, and went back to her pasture.

Since then, I have added much to this improvised group of exercises, and I have eliminated much. With great effort, I have tried to get rid of everything superfluous. With great regret, I have kept only one salute for every ten I have practiced. I have dressed myself in white. I have had multicolored music played that was originally composed for old circuses; I have invited concert pianists to perform. My act lasts twelve minutes, even though my head is filled with centuries of wire walking.

But when I present myself on the ground and grab hold of the rope ladder or cross a public square to begin a Death Walk without a balancing pole, when I see all the equipment on the ground ready to serve me, when I see the orchestra conductor waiting for my signal, I already feel myself to be a wire walker. From that point on, it is a piece of my life that I give or abandon—it depends. The only things I ever remember are walking on the ground, taking hold of the balancing pole for the first crossing, the moment of doubt, and the final salute. I prefer the ground to be flat, uniform, uncluttered, and clean; and I make sure that the spectators have been moved out of the way.

The rest does not belong to me.

It lives in the thousands of hands that will applaud. When I hear the sound of those hands, I am the only one who knows that in the middle of my performance, when I lie down without my balancing pole, my chest in a sky of spotlights, or my heart open to the wind in an outdoor theater, I am next to the gates of Paradise.

REHEARSAL

Stop your normal practicing.

Keep doing walks until your leg breathes and your foot becomes a part of the wire.

Break down each element of your performance in any order you choose and examine it harshly. If the quality is good, repeat it simply as many times as necessary: you must imprint an irreproachable movement on the cable.

Make even the slightest gesture important; do not dawdle over something that seems right. Forget no part of the act.

You are now ready to rehearse.

Go down and rest. Change your costume. Prepare the music. Decide whether you want a few people to watch. Then, as if someone has just announced your entrance, walk toward the wire quickly and with a sure step.

Give your performance.

Go down, and that's it.

Do not do one more thing after that; do not amuse yourself.

Rehearse your act every day, at the end of each practice session.

And go home looking at the ground, thinking of nothing, nothing at all.

STRUGGLE ON THE WIRE

You must throw yourself onto the wire.

Robledillo became one of the great rope dancers at the end of a whip. His father attached little bells to the wire and would come running whenever it became silent.

The glory of suffering does not interest me.

Besides, I don't believe in anything. Uselessness is the only thing I like.

Limits, traps, impossibilities are indispensable to me. Every day I go out to look for them. I believe the whip is necessary only when it is held by the student, not the teacher.

When you train, you should be outside, on a rough coast, all alone.

To learn what you must, it is important to have been treacherously overturned by the ocean's salty air. To have climbed back up to the wire with a wild leap. To have frozen yourself with rage, to have been hell-bent on keeping your balance in the claws of the wind.

You must have weathered long hours of rain and storm, have cried out with joy after each flash of lightning, have cried cries that could push back the thunder.

You must struggle against the elements to learn that staying on a wire is nothing. What counts is this: to stay straight and stubborn in your madness. Only then will you defeat the secrets of the wire. It is the most precious strength of the high-wire walker.

I have kicked off snow with every step as I walked along a frozen cable.

In other seasons, I have run barefoot over a cable burning with sunlight. I have worked without cavallettis on a big cable. I have continued walking on a cable that was progressively loosening with each step. I have tried to cross a completely loose wire, forcing myself to abandon my great assurance. I have even asked people to shake the installation with ropes, to strike the wire with long bars. . . . With complete horror and shame I have fought not to find myself hanging by one hand from the wire with the balancing pole in the other.

I have put on wooden shoes, boots, unmatched pairs of shoes. I have held my balancing pole at my side like a suitcase; I have weighted it down, lightened it, cut it in half, used it with its point off-center in order to walk leaning to one side. I have waited for darkness, so my balance would be disturbed. I have tried Death Walks that were too steep, I have groped along a greasy cable, I have played with telephone wires and railway cables. I have forced myself to rehearse with music that disgusts me. In secret, I have practiced naked to learn how the muscles work and to feel my own ridiculousness.

And, drunk with alcohol, I have proved that a body that knows what it is doing does not need a mind to lead it. . . . I have picked myself up from each of my experiments even more savagely determined. And if I fell, it was in silence. I did not wait for my shoulder wound to heal to go on with my backward somersaults—again and again and again.

I was not possessed. I was busy winning.

You do not do a true *salto* on a very high cable. You do not wear a blindfold or raise your eyes to the sky without using a balancing pole. You do not do a headstand on a great cable without a balancing pole.

Impossible?

Who is smart enough to prove it?

I tell everyone that I will attempt a crossing from the American to the Canadian side of Niagara Falls—where the water actually falls—and not over the rapids, where all previous crossings have been made. But once on that mile of unknown cable, shaken by the wind that does not stop, wrapped in a cloud of vapor that must be pierced little by little, over the whirlpools of the cataract, listening to all that infernal noise, will I dare? Will I dare to be harder than the sun, more glacial than the snow? Will I dare to enter these pages on high-wire walking without knowing the way out? It is one thing to talk about my controlled experiments. But this?

Man of the Air, illuminate with your blood the Very Rich Hours of your passage among us. Limits exist only in the souls of those who do not dream.

THE WIND

If this man standing at the edge of the seawall has not moved for such a long time, it is because he is looking out at the raging sea and watching the birds attempt to fly over the narrow passage—for no other reason than to intoxicate themselves with pleasure.

The harbor is deserted. The hurricane is approaching.

A mass of liquid wind, engulfed between the two towers, carries everything along with it.

The birds that cross from one wall to the next are sometimes assaulted by gusts that shut their wings with a sudden dry noise, hurling them and crushing them against a rock, where they remain until a higher and blacker wave comes to peel them off and wash them away.

The terns, the gulls—excellent sailors with voices so powerful they can hear each other through storms—have taken refuge high up in the green sky and remain silent.

Why do some of them dive down and pierce the smoking sea water that has now risen up in furious columns?

Why do they clamor and brush against the havoc of wind, dust, and foam—which they know is deadly?

Who urges this cruel-eyed animal to test himself against the storm?

One of them has almost managed to get through the forbidden passage on his back; the torrent pursues him and brings him down with a volley of hail.

Only one has made it. The gale has stripped off a few of his feathers, but he rejoins his companions, and they will make him their leader, crying out his victory until nightfall.

But he, the wire walker of the waves, knows that he was granted a miracle, and he remembers that moment with fear, for tomorrow he will be the one they discover stretched out on the seawall.

His dust feeds the wind that little by little wipes him away. Nothing is stronger than the wind. No one is stronger than the wind.

Not even the courageous bird.

FALLS

A fall from the wire, an accident up above, a failed exercise, a false step—all this comes from a lack of concentration, a badly placed foot, an exuberant overconfidence.

You must never forgive yourself.

The high-wire walker becomes the spectator of his own fall. With wide-open eyes he whirls around the wire—until he is caught by an arm or finds himself hanging by a knee. Without letting go of the balancing pole, he must take advantage of this motion to stand up again and continue the interrupted movement with rejuvenated energy.

More often than not, there will be applause. No one will understand what has happened.

The mistake is to leave without hope, without pride, to throw yourself into a routine you know will fail.

Every thought on the wire leads to a fall.

Accidents caused by equipment must not happen.

Many wire walkers have died in this way. It is stupid. But sometimes the wire slips away from you, because you have put yourself outside the law, outside the law of balance. At such moments, your survival depends on the strength of your instinct.

There are those who allow themselves to be carried away without a struggle. Let them fall!

Others continue to flail their arms and legs above the wire, to beg their eyes not to lose sight of their target. With an avid hand they latch onto the cable at the last instant. Have you ever made a leap of faith toward a distant rope, grabbed hold of a cavalletti in midair?

I waited for my first slip in public. It fortified me, it flooded me with a joyous pride, in the same way a solid clap on the shoulder encourages more than it hurts.

The second slip made me think; I found myself below the wire after completing a movement I had mastered long ago. The third incident was terrifying: I almost fell.

Nevertheless, in my dreams I pursue legendary aerial escapes that will finally do me justice. I, who have everything to lose. For when a man begins to tremble for his life, he begins to lose it.

I demand to be allowed to end my life on the wire. I have the patience of those who have fallen once, and whenever someone tells me of a high-wire walker who fell to the ground and was crushed, I answer:

"He got what he deserved."

For that is clearly the fate and the glory of the aerial acrobat.

GREAT CROSSINGS

For two weeks, the high-wire walker has been camping at the top of the mountain.

It is decided. Today he will determine the anchor points.

Eagles wheel around in the lukewarm air of the gorge. They can see this little character on the peak, pointing to a spot on the facing mountain.

An enormous roll of cable is on its way. The special convoy has reached the first steep curves. It will arrive tomorrow. A thousand meters of degreased, twenty-five-millimeter wire: discovered by miracle. It is the most beautiful thing I have ever touched. It weighs three tons. I am happy.

On one side I will encircle an outcrop of rock that stands as solid as a mill.

On the other side there is no protruberance. I will have to dig a hole and then pour a broad and deep column of concrete, around which the wire will be coiled and then fastened for safety to three large trees lined up behind it.

The reel has been solidly rooted to the ground.

A team of twenty men hauls up the wire, chanting as they pull. The cable advances a few inches each minute.

It snakes along the side of the mountain. It clears the road and passes over the telegraph lines. It must be taken across the lake by high-wire methods, for no motorboat would be strong enough to pull it from one shore to the other. If the cable touches bottom, you can forget about your crossing, since it will wedge in among the rocks and catch hold of the weeds so diligently that even the most powerful machines or the most expert divers will never be able to dislodge it. It is cruel for a high wire to drown. Eventually, it will be dragged down through the forest, where each tree is an obstacle; then it will climb, foot by foot, minute after minute, toward its anchor point. At last, everything is ready.

The cable is fastened on each peak. That takes a day. It runs along the valley floor, imprinting its weight on dead leaves, drawing an almost invisible boundary. This becomes alarming at the edges of the lake. You see the black serpent dive into the water and find it hard to imagine that it will emerge on the other side, coming up into the grass and continuing on its way, marking this corner of earth with the disagreeable stamp of its metal skin. Like an immense trap, waiting to snap.

You begin to pull, aided by the largest hoist in the world—or several strategically placed pulleys—and you see a long gray line lift itself from the ground and rise up, swaying. The wire suddenly stops. A small branch somewhere is blocking it.

When you have moved the branch aside with your hand, the cable will jerk up violently another five yards. Everything will go well until the next incident. If you must go through a pine forest, you can expect an additional ten days of installation work. You will have to bend back every branch of every tree the wire gets tangled in.

Finally, the cable is over the valley. It rises up in stages. You must load the motorcycle-trapeze with two thousand pounds of cavallettis and put them astride the cable one by one, while the wire sways back and forth over a radius of ten meters.

"Tighten it to death," your ears open to every sound. Then collect your thoughts.

On the day of the crossing, you will assign each volunteer his rope—which he will have to hold and pull on with all his strength when you are above him, and which he cannot release until you have come to the next cavalletti.

Even so, the cable will move so much that you will see undulations up ahead of you in the distance. You will have to wait for each one of them to come to you before going on with your walk: feet planted, on the alert.

The sun will draw the grease out of the cable.

The wind will pick up the moment you begin.

You will have forgotten to bring socks for the end of the walk, and so you will have to go barefoot, trying to complete the crossing by grasping the wire between your first two toes at every step.

But you will not be aware of anything that is happening. You will be completely engrossed in your crossing.

Only a man who is a high-wire walker to his very bones would dare to do this.

Once on your way, you are becoming the Man of the Wire, the Magician of High Altitudes: the length of your path will be sacred to you.

When you are above the lake, do not look at the surface of the water, for the movement of the waves will make you lose your balance.

If you manage to succeed, don't boast of it. What you have done is enough in itself.

PERFECTION

Attention! You own the wire, that's true. But the essential thing is to etch movements in the sky, movements so still they leave no trace. The essential thing is simplicity.

That is why the long path to perfection is horizontal.

Its principles are the following:

If you want the High Wire to transform you into a high-wire walker, you must rediscover the classic purity of this game. But first you must master its technique. Too bad for the one who turns it into a chore.

Above the crowd on your wire you will pass. Pass above and no more. You will be forgotten.

You must not hesitate. Nor should you be conscious of the ground. That is both stupid and dangerous.

The feet are placed in the direction of the wire, the eyes set themselves on the horizon.

The horizon is not a point, it is a continent.

In walking, it is the wire that pushes you. You offer your balancing pole to the wire, perfectly horizontal, arms spread wide apart.

Like a bird, a man perches *on* the wire; he does not lean forward, ready to fall. On the contrary, he must make himself comfortable.

Learn your body: the movement of your arms, the breathing of your fingers, the tension of your toes, the position of your chin, the weight of your elbows. Leave nothing to chance.

Chance is a thief that never gets caught.

Eliminate cumbersome exercises. Keep those that transfigure you.

Triumph by seeking out the most subtle difficulties. Reach victory through solitude.

The high-wire walker must rest in the way I have described—and fight in that same way.

Never break the rhythm of a crossing. The cable would start to tremble. For high-wire walking does not mean breathing in unison with the rope, but making sure that this joint breathing does not hinder the breath of the one or the palpitation of the other.

Finally: never fail to attend the performances of high-wire walkers.

Make up your own symbol of perfection. For me, it is throwing away the balancing pole.

With a long and endless gesture, the high-wire walker throws his metal pole far across the sky so that it will not strike the wire, and finds himself alone and helpless, richer and more naked, on a cable made to his own measure. With humility, he now knows he is invincible.

A red velvet wire will be unrolled for him in his dreams. He will move along it brandishing his coat of arms.

FEAR

A void like this is terrifying.

Prisoner of a morsel of space, you will struggle desperately against occult elements: the absence of matter, the smell of balance, vertigo from all sides, and the dark desire to return to the ground, even to fall.

This dizziness is the drama of the rope dance, but that is not what I am afraid of.

After long hours of training, the moment comes when there are no more difficulties. Everything is possible, everything becomes easy. It is at this moment that many have perished. But that, no, that is not at all what I am afraid of.

If an exercise resists me during rehearsal, and if it continues to do so a little more each day, to the point of becoming untenable, I prepare a substitute exercise—in case panic grabs me by the throat during a performance. I approach it with more and more reluctance, come to it slyly, surreptitiously. But I always want to persist, to feel the pride of conquering it. In spite of that, I sometimes give up the struggle. But without any fear. I am never afraid on the wire. I am too busy.

But you are afraid of something. I can hear it in your voice. What is it?

Sometimes the sky grows dark around the wire, the wind rises, the cable gets cold, the audience becomes worried. At those moments I hear screams within myself. The wire has stopped breathing. I, too.

It is a prelude to catastrophe—like a drumroll announcing the most difficult exercise. In waiting to fall in this way, I have sometimes cursed the wire, but it has never made me afraid.

I know, however, that one day, standing at the edge of the platform, this anguish will appear. One hideous day it will be waiting for me at the foot of the rope ladder. It will be useless for me to shake myself, to joke about it. The next day it will be in my dressing room as I am putting on my costume, and my hands will be wet with horror. Then it will join me in my sleep. I will be crushed a thousand times, rebounding in slow motion in a circus ring, absolutely weightless. When I wake up, it will be stuck to me, indelible, never to leave me again.

And of that, dear heaven, I have a terrible fear.

To imagine that one evening I will have to give up the wire in the same way that so many bullfighters have given up the ring and disappeared into life; that I will have to say, "I was afraid, I met Holy Fear, it invaded me and sucked my blood"—I who hope to give the greatest gift a high-wire walker can give: to die on my wire, leaving to men the insult of a smiling death mask; I who shouted to others on their ropes: "Remember that life is short! What could be better than a happy man in flight, in midair? Think of all the things you've never done!"; I, the fragile walker of wires, the tiniest of men, I will turn away to hide my tears—and yes, how afraid I am.

Vary, France, winter 1972

OTHER MARSILIO:EW BOOKS

Rosario Castellanos, *The Book of Lamentations*
translated by Esther Allen

Octavio Paz, *Rappaccini's Daughter*
translated by Sebastian Doggart

OTHER MARSILIO BOOKS FROM THE FRENCH

Jacques Cazotte, *The Devil in Love*
translated by Stephen Sartarelli

Denis Diderot, *The Indiscreet Jewels*
translated by Sophie Hawkes

Pierre Klossowski, *The Baphomet*
translated by Sophie Hawkes and Stephen Sartarelli

Pierre Klossowski, *Diana at her Bath/The Women of Rome*
translated by Sophie Hawkes and Stephen Sartarelli

Michel Leiris, *Nights as Days, Days as Nights*
translated by Richard Sieburth

Raymond Radiguet, *Count D'Orgel's Ball*
translated by Anna Cancogni